"I may never marry at all," Abby said, her voice sounding noncommittal.

Jakob jerked his head up, blinking at her in surprise. Not marry? Ever? The idea was alien to him.

"You should marry. It is what *Gott* would want."

"I know you really believe that. I'm not so sure anymore."

Hmm, he didn't like the sound of that. And yet, how could he fault Abby when he was shunning marriage for himself?

"Of course you will marry one day," he said.

She smiled and Jakob felt a new awareness sweep over him. Abby wasn't just a girl from his past. She was now a beautiful woman. He hurried to his feet and moved away. He couldn't face the disloyalty he felt toward his late wife. Never once had he been tempted by another woman.

Until now.

He was definitely attracted to her, but that wasn't enough. After everything Abby had been through, she deserved for someone to adore her.

But that someone couldn't be him.

Leigh Bale is a *Publishers Weekly* bestselling author. She is the winner of the prestigious Golden Heart® Award and is a finalist for the Gayle Wilson Award of Excellence and the Booksellers' Best Award. The daughter of a retired US forest ranger, she holds a BA in history. Married in 1981 to the love of her life, Leigh and her professor husband have two children and two grandkids. You can reach her at leighbale.com.

Visit the Author Profile page at Harlequin.com for more titles.

Runaway
Amish Bride

Leigh Bale

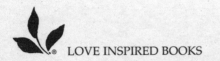

Recycling programs
for this product may
not exist in your area.

LOVE INSPIRED BOOKS

ISBN-13: 978-1-335-42829-5

Runaway Amish Bride

www.Harlequin.com

Printed in U.S.A.

...See that ye love one another
with a pure heart fervently.
—*1 Peter* 1:22

Chapter One

Abigail Miller sat primly on the edge of a tall-backed chair and stared at Jakob Fisher, his long fingers clenched around the letters Abby had given him.

He paced the length of the spacious living room in his home, his blue chambray shirt stretched taut across his overly broad shoulders and muscular arms. Even his black suspenders looked tight against his solid back. He had just arrived from working in the fields, and his plain trousers and black boots had dust on them. His dark hair was slightly damp and curled against the nape of his neck, confirming that the April weather was unseasonably warm. His straw hat sat on a table where he'd carelessly tossed it twenty minutes earlier. His high forehead furrowed as he scowled at his mother.

"I can't believe you told this woman I would marry her," he muttered.

Naomi Fisher met her son's gaze. She sat beside Bishop Yoder on the sofa, her hands in her lap. The friction in the room was palpable. Abby couldn't help wishing she had never come to Colorado. Even the abuse she had suffered back home in Ohio at the hands of her father and elder brother was preferable to this humiliating scene.

"I didn't make the offer, *mein sohn*. As you can see from his letters, your father did this, just before he died." Naomi spoke in a quiet, matter-of-fact voice, her expression calm but resolute.

Jakob handed the letters back to Abby. Several pages escaped her grasp and drifted to the floor. She bent over to gather them up, then placed them neatly inside her purse. They were like a shameful reminder that she'd done something wrong, but she hadn't. She'd merely agreed to what she thought was a marriage proposal.

"Did you know what *Daed* had done?" Jakob asked.

"*Ne*, I didn't know anything about it. Not until today. I just thought Abby was coming to Colorado to visit us," Naomi said.

The bishop cleared his voice. "Your *vad-*

der told me of his plans, although he led me to believe that you had agreed to the offer of marriage. I thought it was all arranged. I'm sorry that I didn't speak with you about it before now."

Jakob stopped dead and stared at the man. "*Ne*, I knew nothing. Why didn't *Daed* tell me about it? I never would have agreed to such a scheme."

Abby flinched at the irritation in his voice. She felt devious, as though she had plotted behind Jakob's back. She shifted her weight, wishing she could disappear. Wishing she were anywhere but here. She had arrived by bus only two hours earlier. Naomi, Bishop Yoder and his wife, Sarah, had been at the station to meet her. After traveling for twenty-six hours, Abby was hungry, exhausted and relieved to see a friendly face. She'd climbed into the back of the bishop's buggy and he had driven her here, to the Fishers' farm just nine miles outside town. She thought she was coming here to marry Jakob, the only man she'd ever trusted. Now, she realized she'd made a huge mistake.

"I'm already married. Susan is my wife," Jakob said, his voice sounding hoarse with emotion.

Abby jerked her head up at this information. Jakob had a wife? When had that happened?

Obviously, Jakob hadn't known about his father's offer until this morning. Even among the Amish, an arranged marriage was considered old-fashioned. But Abby had suffered a lifetime of abuse at the hands of her father and elder brother, Simon. Desperate to escape, she had agreed to come to Colorado. Naomi had been childhood friends with her mother. Fourth cousins, to be exact. Abby had been a girl when they'd left Ohio, but she still remembered them.

Naomi lifted her head, her eyes shimmering with moisture. "Susan is gone, but your children still need a *mamm*. Perhaps that is why your *vadder* contacted Abby and told her to come here."

"My children have you to mother them. They don't need anyone else. And it wasn't *Daed's* place to find me a wife," Jakob said.

Naomi nodded. "You are right, of course. But Reuben is so angry all the time. He's becoming uncontrollable. Yesterday, his schoolteacher told me he put a frog in her desk drawer. It jumped out and nearly scared her to death. And he's constantly teasing Ruby and making her cry."

Abby listened intently. He had children, too! Reuben and Ruby. Those must be their names. And knowing that Reuben was picking on Ruby made Abby's defenses go up like a kite flying high. She couldn't help feeling instantly protective of the girl.

Jakob released a heavy sigh of frustration. "I will speak with him again."

"That's just it. He won't listen. He needs a *mamm*. So does Ruby. They need a complete *familye*," Naomi said.

Sitting next to the bishop wearing a black traveling bonnet, Sarah Yoder nodded her agreement.

A sick feeling settled in Abby's stomach. She hadn't known any of this information. That Jakob had been married before and had two children. That was more than she'd bargained for.

"I didn't know." She spoke in a quiet voice, needing to understand exactly what she was getting herself into. At his father's urging, she had agreed to marry Jakob, not become an instant mother.

Jakob turned, his eyes widening, as if he'd forgotten she was here. "What didn't you know?"

She swallowed, gathering her courage. "That you were married before and have *kinder*."

"*Ach*, it's true." He looked away, his gestures filled with impatience.

A dark, heavy silence followed.

"Jakob is a widower. Susan died in childbirth sixteen months ago," Naomi explained in a gentle tone.

Oh, dear. Jakob's father had neglected to mention that in his letters. Abby couldn't help wondering what the man had been playing at. Had he hoped to get her here and then convince her to become a stepmother to Jakob's children? Why hadn't he told her the truth before she traveled across the country? Since the man had died suddenly a few weeks earlier, she would never know. It had taken her all that time to convince her brother to let her come here, and now it seemed a wasted effort.

"How old are your *kinder*?" she asked.

Jakob raked a hand through his short hair, showing his annoyance. "Reuben is seven and Ruby is five."

"I didn't know anything about them," she said.

Now what? She hadn't expected this. No, not at all.

The Western United States seemed strange and isolated to Abby, but it offered a chance at freedom. To begin a new life of peace and happiness. At the age of twenty-four, she should have already wed. But frankly, her father and brother had soured her toward all men.

Except one.

A rush of memory filled Abby's mind. She'd

been twelve years old when Simon was beating her with a heavy stick…doing what he'd seen their father do so many times before. Up until then, Jakob had been friends with Simon. The two boys were both fifteen years old. Jakob had been working with his *daed* in a nearby field. When he'd seen what was happening, he'd marched through the tall wheat, jerked the stick out of Simon's hand and broken it over his bended knee. Simon had been furious that Jakob would interfere, but he hadn't dared challenge him. Jakob was bigger, stronger and fiercer. He'd shielded Abby, giving her time to flee.

When Jakob's *familye* had migrated to Colorado a year later, Abby never forgot his kindness. And every time her father or brother beat her, she thought about Jakob and his compassion. It was the only reason she had agreed to marry him. But now, she had a dilemma. If she returned to Ohio, she'd be forced to live in Simon's household, where she had no doubt the abuse would continue. And she couldn't stand that. No, not ever again. But maybe there was another option.

"I understand a marriage will not work between us." She spoke softly, her hands trembling.

Jakob tilted his head to the side. "What did you say?"

She forced herself to meet his dark, angry eyes and repeated herself. "There has obviously been a horrible misunderstanding. But now that I am here, is it possible that I might work for you? Surely you need help on the farm. I am eager not to return to Ohio. Please. Don't send me back there. Let me stay and work here."

She hated that she must resort to begging, but life was harsh for an Amish woman alone in the world. She didn't want to return to the misery waiting for her in Ohio, but neither did she want to abandon her faith for a life among the *Englisch*. She could work to make her way, if only Jakob would agree.

"I see no reason why you must leave, especially when you just got here," Bishop Yoder said. "Our district is anxious to bring new members into its fold, to increase our settlement. There are not enough women of our faith to marry our young men. You would be a great asset to our congregation."

Abby understood the implication of his words. If Jakob wouldn't marry her, then someone else would because they were in short supply of Amish women. But what they didn't know was that Abby would never agree to marry any of them. The fact that Jakob's father had misguided her only confirmed her belief that most men could not be trusted and they used women only to get what they wanted.

Naomi nodded eagerly. "Of course, you must stay. We can find room for you here. There's always work to be done, and we really could use more help. The bishop's wife runs a bakery in town, and we contribute baked goods on consignment. In fact, I have to make a delivery in town tomorrow morning."

Sarah nodded eagerly. "*Ja*, that is true."

"You could also assist me with keeping an eye on the *kinder*," Naomi continued.

Abby didn't mind looking after children, but she felt a little odd tending Jakob's kids. It was preferable to returning to Ohio. Everyone seemed eager for her to remain here. Everyone except Jakob.

"I would like that very much," Abby said.

In unison, they all turned to look at Jakob. Their eyes were filled with hope as they silently awaited his verdict. For the first time in Abby's life, it felt good to be wanted for a change, even if it was just Naomi, the bishop and Sarah who wanted her.

Jakob blinked, regarding them all as if he were a cornered rabbit facing a pride of mountain lions. Panicked and desperate. Abby held her breath, silently praying he agreed to let her stay.

* * *

Jakob took a deep breath, then released it slowly. He tried to calm his racing heart and troubled mind. Right now, he didn't know what to think. Confusion fogged his brain. Too much grief had struck his *familye* lately. First, his beloved wife, Susan, had died in childbirth. Then *Daed* had died of a heart attack a few weeks ago. But why had *Daed* written to Abby and said that Jakob had agreed to marry her? It didn't make sense.

Between the farm and his furniture-making business, Jakob already had more responsibilities than he could handle effectively without a wife. Though he tried, he had little time to comfort his grieving children. *Mamm* and his elderly grandfather had filled in the gaps. They'd been a great deal of help, but they were also still in mourning. He was responsible for each of them. To cope with his loss, he had buried himself in his work. It was easier to pretend that Susan was still alive, waiting for him at home at the end of each day. That his father was available anytime he needed advice or help with his labors. That they were a whole and happy *familye* again.

But they weren't.

He definitely could use assistance on the farm, but not a wife. Never that. He would not allow Bishop Yoder or *Mamm* to pressure him into marrying again. It hurt too much. But what should he do about Abigail Miller?

He reminded himself that he wasn't the only one who had been duped by his *daed*. After reading his father's letters to Abby, he realized she hadn't known that he was a widower with two young children to raise. Right now, they were with *Dawdi* Zeke, their great-grandfather, and not here to witness this difficult conversation. Reuben was still so angry that his *mudder* and grandfather had died. He and Ruby couldn't understand what had happened to their world.

Neither could Jakob. It seemed that *Gott* had abandoned them, and he didn't know why.

"I suppose we could make room for you here in the house, at least until you decide what you'd like to do. I can stay with *Dawdi* Zeke, so that there is no appearance of impropriety," he said.

There. That was good. His offer provided an immediate solution to Abby's needs without making any long-term commitments. And by staying with *Dawdi*, it would remove Jakob from the house so that no one could accuse him of indecency with a woman who wasn't his wife. Of course, he'd still be taking his meals here in the house, but with Naomi and *Dawdi's* presence, no member of his congregation could accuse him of being inappropriate.

"*Dawdi* Zeke?" Abby asked.

"My grandfather."

She nodded. "*Danke*. I am grateful to accept your offer."

She released a quiet sigh and looked away, her startling blue eyes filled with relief. He couldn't blame her. He remembered her *familye* well and could guess her reason for not wanting to return to them. *Mamm* had told him that her father had died a few years earlier, which left her to the questionable mercy of Simon. Jakob had no doubt the boy had grown up to be a cruel man just like his father, and he hated the thought of sending Abby back to him.

A clatter sounded outside the open window. Jakob stepped over to peer out and saw Reuben racing across the lawn toward the barn. A bucket was overturned in the flower bed, as though it had been used as a step stool. The boy's footprints were embedded in the damp soil, and he had tromped on Naomi's petunias.

Hmm. No doubt the little scamp had been listening in on their conversation. Jakob had no idea how much the boy had overheard, but he would have to deal with that later.

"*Wundervoll*. I am so glad we have come to an agreement. Abby will remain here, then."

Bishop Yoder slapped his hands against his thighs and stood to signal his departure. Sarah rose also, smiling wide.

Naomi hopped up and escorted them out onto the front porch. "I appreciate your being here today."

"Any time. Let me know how things go…" The bishop's voice faded as the screen door clapped closed behind him.

Jakob turned and faced Abby. She'd been a young girl when he saw her last. Young, quiet and afraid. Now, she was an attractive, fully grown woman with magnetic blue eyes; smooth, pale skin; and golden-blond hair. Her light blue dress and matching cape looked perfectly starched, though her skirts were slightly wrinkled from her travels. She still looked quiet, still afraid. The complete opposite of his outspoken wife. Susan had been olive-skinned with dark hair, freckles, hazel eyes and an overly long nose. She wasn't what most people would call beautiful, but she'd been kind and energetic, and Jakob had loved her dearly.

Correction. He still loved her. He always would. And he had no room in his heart to love another woman. Not ever again.

Now, Abby sat with her battered suitcase resting beside her on the hardwood floor. Her shoulders sagged with weariness. Still wearing her black travel bonnet, she appeared tuckered out and in need of some time by herself. She reached up and slid an errant strand of flaxen hair back into her *kapp*, looking lost and all alone in the world.

A twinge of compassion pinched his heart.

"*Koom*. I will show you to your room." Without waiting for her, Jakob scooped up her bag and headed toward the back stairs. She followed. He could hear the delicate tapping of her sensible black shoes behind him.

Upstairs, he pushed the door wide to offer Abby admittance. She stepped inside and looked around the tidy room. It included a simple double bed, a nightstand on each side with tall gas lamps, a chest of drawers, a wooden chair and an armoire. The oak furnishings were beautiful but plain. Jakob had crafted the wood himself as a wedding gift for his new bride. They complemented the lovely blue Dresden Plate quilt that covered the bed. The design included small gold hearts at the corner of each quilt block. A matching braided rag rug covered the bare wood floor. Susan had made the quilt, rug and plain curtains hanging across the window. She'd claimed that the hearts on the quilt were a whimsical reminder of their love. And though pride was not something Jakob should allow himself, he couldn't help feeling just a bit of *Hochmut* for her skill in making them.

Abby turned, her gaze riveted to the far corner of the room where a rocking cradle sat awaiting a little occupant. She made a small sound of sympathy in the back of her throat, her eyes filled with sadness. He'd made the cradle for his new child. As he looked at the empty mattress, a wave of lonely helplessness crashed over him. All his hopes and dreams seemed to have died with Susan and their unborn child. He should have removed it by now but hadn't been able to let go of the past. Packing the cradle off to the barn would seem like burying his wife and child all over again. So he'd left it here, a constant reminder of all he'd lost.

He looked away, trying to squelch the pain. Setting Abby's suitcase on the floor with a dull thud, he walked to the armoire and reached inside. It took only a moment to gather up his clothes. He didn't have much, just what he needed.

Abby watched him quietly, her delicate forehead crinkled in a frown. Her gaze lifted to a hook on the wall where his black felt hat rested. He scooped it up, feeling out of place in his own home. Having this woman see the room he had shared with his wife seemed much too personal.

Abby looked at him, her eyes creased with compassion, and he felt as though she could see deep inside his tattered heart.

"This is your room," she said.

It was a statement, not a question.

"*Ja*, but it is yours to use now. I will join *Dawdi* in the *dawdy haus*. He turned ninety-three last month and is quite frail, but he still lives alone now that his wife is gone."

The *dawdy haus* was a tiny building next to the main house with a bedroom, bathroom, small living area and kitchenette. It included a front porch with two rocking chairs, although *Dawdi* Zeke didn't do much idle sitting even though he was so old. The cottage was the Amish version of an old folks' home, except that they cared for their elderly grandparents instead of turning them over to strangers. Jakob had no doubt the man would be happy to let him live with him for the time being.

"I'm sorry to chase you out of your room," Abby said.

He shrugged. "It's no problem, although *Dawdi* Zeke does snore a bit."

He showed a half smile, but she just stared at him, totally missing his attempt at humor.

"We will eat supper soon. Come down when you are ready." With one last glance around the room, he closed the door.

Alone for a moment, he stood on the landing, his thoughts full of turmoil. He didn't want Abby here, but the situation wasn't her fault. She'd come to Colorado in good faith. No doubt she was hoping for a better life than what she'd had with her own *familye*. He knew how he would feel if Reuben were beating little Ruby with a stick, and he made a mental note to speak with his son right after supper. He'd feel like a failure if one of his children grew up to be cruel and abusive. He couldn't marry Abby, but neither could he turn his back on her in her time of need. If nothing else, he could shelter her. The Lord would expect no less.

Turning, he descended the creaking stairs and entered the wide kitchen. *Mamm* stood in front of the gas stove, stirring a pot of bubbling soup. Strands of gray hair had escaped her *kapp* and hung around her flushed cheeks. She looked tired, but he knew she'd never complain. It wasn't their way.

The fragrant aroma of freshly baked biscuits wafted through the air. *Mamm* paused, looking at his armful of clothes. Her gaze lifted to his face, as if assessing his mood.

"Jakob, I'm so sorry. Your *vadder* never should have interfered..."

He held up a hand. She hadn't been privy to his father's plans and it wasn't her fault, but he didn't want to discuss it any further. "Abby is welcome in our home until she wishes to leave, but I am not marrying her or any woman. Not ever. Now, I'm going to get *Dawdi* and the children so we can eat. I heard Abby's stomach rumbling and believe she is hungry. We should feed her before I complete the evening chores."

With that final word on the subject, he stepped out onto the back porch and walked past the yellow daffodils Susan had planted the first year they'd been married. He saw her presence everywhere on the farm. In the garden where she'd grown huge beefsteak tomatoes in spite of the short growing season, and in his children's eyes. They both looked so much like their mother that he could never forget. Nor did he want to.

No, he definitely would never marry again. It was that simple.

Chapter Two

"What's taking her so long?"

Abby heard the impatient words as she reached the bottom of the stairs. The voice sounded grouchy, like it came from a young boy. No doubt Reuben was hungry and she was keeping him waiting.

Smoothing one hand over her apron, she subconsciously patted her white *kapp* before entering the kitchen. A gas lamp hung from the high ceiling, filling the room with warm light. Through the window above the sink, Abby saw the dusky sky painted with fingers of pink and gold. The warmth from the woodstove embraced her chilled arms and hands along with the delicious aromas of food. She hadn't eaten since the day before and her stomach grumbled as she took another step.

"I'm sorry to keep you waiting." She stood

in the doorway, gazing at the occupants of the room.

Two children, a boy and girl with identical chins and eyes, stared back at her. The boy sat on Jakob's left with the girl next to him. As Naomi turned from the woodstove with a plate of steaming biscuits, Jakob and an elderly man scooted back their chairs and rose from their places at the head of each end of the long table. Their respect was not lost on Abby, and she stared at them in surprise. No one had ever stood up for her in her father's home.

"Here she is." Naomi spoke in a lilting voice as she showed Abby a happy smile.

"*Willkomm* to our home." The elderly man hobbled over and took Abby's hands in his.

This must be *Dawdi* Zeke, Jakob's grandfather. His long beard was white as snow, his face lined with deep creases. A pair of wire-rimmed spectacles sat on the bridge of his nose, his gray eyes sparkling with humor and the experience of a long life. As Abby looked at him, she found nothing to fear.

"*Danke,*" she said, conscious Jakob was watching her.

"Sit here." Naomi pointed to a chair on Jakob's right.

As Abby rounded the table, the two children

stared at her…the girl with open curiosity, the boy with open hostility.

"But that's *Mamm's* seat," the boy said.

Abby hesitated, her hand resting along the high back of the wooden chair.

Jakob's mouth tightened and he didn't say a word, but his dark eyes mirrored his son's disapproval.

"I can sit here." Abby sat across from Ruby instead, not wanting to stir up any more animosity.

In spite of her effort to please him, Reuben gave a gigantic huff and rested his elbows on the table, his chin cradled in the palms of his hands. He eyed her as though she were a stinky dog that shouldn't be allowed in the house.

"Sit up straight and mind your manners," Naomi told him with slightly raised eyebrows.

The boy did as asked, but his glare stayed firmly in place. Abby tried not to squirm beneath his unfriendly gaze and decided that ill-mannered children should be ignored. She instead focused on Ruby and was rewarded for her effort. The girl grinned, showing a bottom tooth missing in front.

"You're pretty," Ruby said.

"*Danke.* So are you," Abby said, feeling the heat of a blush suffuse her face. She wasn't used to such praise, even from a child.

"You're not our *mamm*. You never will be." Reuben blurted the words angrily, then scooted back his chair and raced out of the room. The chair toppled to the floor with a loud clatter.

Abby flinched.

"Reuben!" Jakob called, but the boy kept going.

Abby blinked, not knowing what to say.

"I'll go speak with him." Jakob stood and walked around the table to set the fallen chair back up, then left the room.

Abby stared at her hands. It was obvious that Reuben didn't like her. That he felt threatened by her. And if she were going to stay here, she must figure out a way to show him that she meant no harm.

"Where did Reuben and *Daed* go?" Ruby asked, her little chin quivering.

"Reuben isn't feeling well. Your *vadder* will look after him, but he will be fine," *Dawdi* said.

The girl accepted this without further complaint.

"It'll be all right," Naomi whispered and patted Abby's shoulder, then set the biscuits in the middle of the table and took her seat.

Dawdi smiled at each person in turn, as though trying to bring a better mood back to the room.

"Let us pray and give thanks to the Lord for

the bounty we enjoy each day." He waited patiently for them to bow their heads.

His words warmed Abby's heart. She couldn't help comparing Zeke's actions with those of her father and brother. Back home, if she didn't hurry, she could find herself receiving a solid smack with the back of her brother's hand. There was never any tolerance waiting for children or women in his home.

In unison, they closed their eyes. Silently in her mind, Abby recited the Lord's Prayer from the New Testament. Then, she quickly thanked *Gott* for bringing her safely to Colorado and asked that He might comfort Reuben and help her make a successful life here. Everyone at the table released a quick exhale, and Ruby reached for the biscuits. Naomi hopped out of her chair and hurried to pour glasses of milk for them. The woman bustled around, seeing to everyone else's needs. Abby stood up to help, but Naomi pushed her back into her seat.

"You've had a long enough day. Just sit and eat your meal."

Feeling frazzled and exhausted, Abby sat down.

"How was your ride into town on the bus?" *Dawdi* asked as Naomi ladled thick soup into his bowl.

"It was long and tiring, but I saw some amazing scenery on my journey. Your mountains are so tall. I'm glad to be here," Abby said truthfully.

"I'd like to ride on a bus someday, but we only travel by horse and buggy," little Ruby said.

"Unless we need to travel a great distance, as Abby has done. Then we would take the bus," *Dawdi* said.

"Then I want to go on a long trip one day. Then I can ride the bus," she said.

Dawdi smiled. "I'm sure you will, one day."

Jakob returned a short time later with Reuben in tow. The boy sniffled, his face and eyes red from crying. He paused beside Abby's chair and stared at the toes of his bare feet.

"Go on. Do as you were told," Jakob urged the boy.

Reuben heaved a tremulous sigh. "I'm sorry for what I said earlier."

Overcome by compassion for the motherless boy, Abby couldn't resist reaching out and squeezing his arm. The moment she did so, she felt him tense beneath her fingertips, and she removed her hand. He might have apologized, but she could tell he wasn't really sorry.

"It's all right. No one could ever replace your good *mudder*," she said.

He glanced at her face, as though surprised by her words. Then a glint of suspicion flashed in his eyes. He didn't say anything as his lips pursed and he took his seat at the table. Keeping his gaze downcast, he ate his meal in silence. And then a thought occurred to Abby. Surely Jakob wouldn't have beaten the boy into submission. She knew many Amish parents adhered to the *spare the rod, spoil the child* mantra. But not Jakob. Not the man she'd known and trusted all these years. He wouldn't do such a thing. Would he? She hadn't seen him in years and didn't really know him anymore. Maybe he'd changed. And the thought that she might be the cause of Reuben suffering a spanking, or worse, made her feel sick inside. If so, he now had a viable reason to hate her. And if Jakob had struck the boy, she wouldn't be able to like him either. Maybe it was a blessing they would not be marrying.

She nibbled a biscuit but had suddenly lost her appetite.

Jakob lifted a spoonful of soup to his mouth. He chewed for a moment, then swallowed. "I'll start plowing the fields tomorrow, but I don't want to plant the feed corn too soon. We could still get a killing frost."

"I think we're safe now." *Dawdi* spoke between bites. "We can plant anytime. But tomorrow morning, you should go with the women to the bakery. They've got a lot of heavy items to carry and they'll need your strength. I can stay here and finish staining that oak hutch for Jason Crawley."

"But the day after tomorrow is the Sabbath. I won't be able to plant then," Jakob said.

Dawdi shrugged. "We can plant on Monday. That is soon enough. It'll give us a couple of extra days since you're worried about frost. It shouldn't keep us from having a bountiful harvest."

Jakob nodded, accepting his grandfather's advice without protest. *Dawdi* Zeke might be old, but he knew what he was talking about.

Jakob glanced briefly at Abby, and her senses went on high alert. She felt as though he could see deep inside her, but she couldn't understand why he made her so jittery. Perhaps it was because she doubted him now, just as she doubted all men. Was it possible the compassionate boy she had known had grown up to be abusive like her brother?

"*Ja*, you are right. I should drive *Mamm* into town," Jakob said. "She is low on flour, and I don't want her to lift the heavy bags. We will drop off her breads and pies at the bakery, then go to the store and purchase the other supplies she needs."

"*Ach*, I can lift those bags just fine," Naomi said.

"I can help. I'm strong and can do the lifting, too," Abby offered, wanting to earn her keep.

"Absolutely not. Naomi will be glad to have your help with the baking, but let Jakob lift the bags of flour," Zeke said.

Abby nodded, returning the man's warm smile. Back home, her brother expected her to do heavy work. In spite of the aches and pains in her muscles and joints, she'd learned not to ask him for help. Even with Reuben's outburst, it felt so good to be sitting here, having a *fami-lye* meal and a normal discussion. It was her first day in Riverton and she was beyond grateful to be here.

She tasted her savory chicken noodle soup, and her hunger took over. Even though she was nervous, she ate her fill, enjoying strawberry preserves spread across her warm biscuits. They consumed one of Naomi's schnitz apple pies for dessert. And when the meal ended, the men scooted back their chairs.

"I will be out in the barn," Jakob announced.

Abby realized his evening chores must have been interrupted because of her arrival, and she felt the heat of embarrassment stain her cheeks. Normally, the majority of farm chores were completed before sitting down to the evening meal.

"I'll help you," Abby said, wanting to do her part.

"No need. Tomorrow, you can work. Tonight, you should rest," Jakob said.

Dawdi walked around the table and leaned down to kiss Naomi on the forehead. "Another delicious meal, my dear."

Likewise, Jakob kissed his mother's cheek. *"Danke, Mamm."*

"Gern geschehen." Naomi smiled with satisfaction. She squeezed *Dawdi's* hand but looked at her son. "Don't let him overdo or lift anything heavy out there."

Jakob nodded obediently. "I won't."

Dawdi pursed his lips. "You can both stop mothering me. I've worked all my life and raised a *familye*. I'll lift anything I want. I'm not a *boppli*."

No, he definitely wasn't a baby. He continued murmuring as he hobbled toward the door. Although his words sounded terse, his tone was light and pleasant. Abby knew they were just worried about the elderly man, but she wasn't used to this kind of loving banter and couldn't be sure.

"I would never question your skills, *Dawdi.*

You know more about farming than anyone in the state," Jakob said, resting his arm across his grandfather's feeble shoulders.

"I'm glad I'm still good for something," Zeke replied with a laugh.

Abby stared in shock. Growing up, she'd never seen this kind of affection nor gratitude shown in her home. Was this normal in most Amish households, or just this one? It seemed so alien to Abby, and yet she wished she had been raised this way.

"I'll gather the eggs." Reuben stuffed half a biscuit into his mouth before pushing away from the table.

"I want to help, too." Ruby hopped out of her chair, and both children quickly carried their dishes to the sink before kissing their grandmother. Then they raced outside with the men.

Naomi released a huge sigh and finally sat at the table. She cupped her face with her hands, breathing hard.

"Are you all right?" Abby asked.

The woman nodded and sat back, seeming to relax now that her *familye* had been cared for. "I'm fine. There's just a lot to do."

She reached for a bowl and filled it with soup for herself. She began eating, and Abby thought she was overdoing.

"Now that I'm here, I can help take some of the load off you," Abby said.

Naomi smiled. "*Ja*, I'm so glad to have you here, my dear."

Again, the woman's words warmed Abby's heart. "The *kinder* are so eager to assist with the work."

She was thinking of home again. She'd never been opposed to hard work, but she hated being anywhere near her father or brother. Surely Reuben wouldn't be eager to help in the barn if his dad was inclined to beating him and Ruby.

Naomi nodded. "They are good children. I hope you know Reuben didn't mean any harm by what he said earlier."

"*Ja*, I understand that he has suffered a great loss. You all have."

Naomi showed a sad smile. "I am sorry for how this has turned out with Jakob. You must be very disappointed not to be marrying him."

Abby shrugged. "Not really. I am content not to be married. And I'm so grateful to be able to stay here with you. I promise not to be a burden. I'll earn my keep."

"Don't worry about that. I like having a house full of *familye*. But you should marry one day. It's a lot of work but also brings boundless joy. Losing my husband has been difficult, but we had many wonderful years together and I have my grandchildren to enjoy now. But I am very worried about Reuben and Jakob."

"How many children do you have?" Abby asked, standing so she could clear the table.

"Five, including Jakob, who is the eldest. They are all grown and married now. Three of them live in the Westcliffe area and come to visit us now and then. Colorado isn't like Ohio, where all of our *familye* lives close by. Here, we are spread far apart, but we are glad to have affordable land. There is plenty of room to grow. We can have a better future here. My daughter Ruth and her husband live here in Riverton. You'll meet them at church on Sunday. She is expecting her first child in August. Then I will have eight grandchildren to love. I hope to have many more."

Abby smiled at the thought, wishing she could have children someday. A husband and a large *familye* that loved each other had always been her dream. But children of her own would require marriage, which didn't appear to be in her future. Although it wasn't quite the same, she would just have to care for other people's children. Starting with Reuben and Ruby.

"How nice that your *familye* is growing so much. You must be very pleased," she said.

Naomi set her spoon in her empty bowl and pushed back from the table with a sigh. "I am.

It is good to have a large *familye* in my old age, but I would feel better to see *mein sohn* happily married again. I can understand why my husband wrote to tell you that Jakob would marry you. The Amish settlements in Colorado are just beginning to grow. Bishop Yoder fears without enough women, our young men might start marrying outside our faith. I'm sure that is one reason he was eager for you to remain here with us."

Abby didn't respond to that. She thought it was better to let the topic die. And yet, she'd had such great expectations. Now, she wasn't so sure.

"Is *Dawdi* Zeke your father?" she asked.

Naomi nodded. "He is kind, yet firm in his convictions. He's lived a long, happy life. Jakob is just like him, although you wouldn't know it lately. He's still hurting over losing his wife. But one day, he will realize that *Gott* wants him to keep going and to be happy. That he cannot live in the past."

Abby agreed, yet she realized how difficult it must be for Jakob. He'd lost two vital people he loved very much, and she envied that love. How she wished someone in the world loved her the way Jakob loved Susan. Abby was so traumatized by her life in Ohio that she was desperate to leave it behind, yet Jakob wanted to cling to the past. She realized neither mindset was healthy, but she had no idea how to overcome the problem.

"Now, tell me about Ohio and our old home. Who has married recently and who has had new babies? Tell me all the news." Naomi stood and walked to the kitchen sink.

Abby willingly complied, drying the dishes while Naomi washed. They laughed and chatted as they worked, soon having the room cleaned up and plans made for tomorrow's meals. That didn't diminish the worries in Abby's mind. She was a stranger in a new home. She'd come here to get married, but surely things had worked out for the best. The Lord knew of her needs and would care for her. She must have faith. Jakob had let her stay, and she didn't dare ask for more. So why did she feel an unexplainable sense of disappointment deep inside her heart?

The air smelled of a combination of cattle and clean straw. The horses were inside their stalls, blissfully munching on hay. The sun had all but faded in the western sky, highlighting the fields with shadows of dark purple and gray. Jakob lit a kerosene lamp and set it on the railing. He loved this late time of day, when he'd almost finished his work and could go inside and read or talk with his *familye* before the fire-place. But lately, he found no peace of mind.

Sitting on a three-legged stool, he set a clean bucket beneath one of their three cows.

"Abby is a sweet young woman, don't you agree?" *Dawdi* Zeke asked.

Jakob paused in his milking and glanced over at his grandfather. It was a good thing that Reuben and Ruby were outside feeding the pigs. It might have been a mistake, but he'd told *Dawdi* about his father's letters to Abby and that he had refused to marry her.

"She is a nice enough person I suppose," he said.

Dawdi leaned against the side of the cow he was milking. He sat at a hunched angle, indicating his arthritis was bothering him again. His bucket was almost filled with frothy white milk or Jakob might have tried to get him to go inside. He gave his fragile grandfather as few chores to do as possible. The *familye* couldn't stand to lose anyone else right now.

"Susan was a sweet woman, too," *Dawdi* said. "It was a shame to lose her. But it's been over a year and it's time for you to live again. If you open your heart to love, you will find more joy than you ever thought possible."

Open his heart to love? Jakob didn't know how anymore. Even if he could do it, he didn't want to try. When he'd married Susan, he'd locked his heart to all others. What if he loved another woman and lost her, too? He couldn't stand to go through that pain a second time, nor did he want to put his children through it again.

"I'll never love anyone the way I loved Susan," he said.

"True. Susan was unique and you loved her for who she was. But Abby is unique, too. She'll bring some man a lot of happiness. If you decide not to love again, then that's the way it'll be. But it doesn't have to be like that. It's your choice."

"It wasn't my choice when Susan died. I can't tell my heart what to feel or who to love," Jakob said.

How could he tell his heart to stop loving Susan and start loving another woman? He couldn't shut it off and on. It wasn't possible.

"*Ja*, you can. All you have to do is stop being angry at *Gott* and start living in the present instead of the past. Look for ways to feel joy and you'll find it." With a final nod, *Dawdi* stood slowly and carried his bucket out of the milking room. He set the container on top of the rough-hewn counter. When he turned, he staggered but caught himself against a beam of timber.

"*Dawdi!* Are you all right?" Jakob stood so

fast that he almost kicked his bucket over. A dollop of frothy white milk sloshed over the pail.

"I'm all right." *Dawdi* Zeke held up a hand to reassure him.

Jakob was still worried. With his father passing away so recently, they were shorthanded. To take up the slack, *Dawdi* Zeke had been overdoing, but he would never complain. Jakob would make a point of doing the milking earlier for a few days, to give his grandfather a rest.

He glanced at the buckets, mentally calculating how many gallons of milk they would have tonight. He knew *Mamm* would separate the cream later, to make butter and other tasty fillings for the pastries she sold at the bakery in town. During the past few years of drought, the extra income she brought in had been a blessing. With Abby's help, they should be able to increase their production.

Jakob lowered his head and continued with his task. Yes, Abby was a sweet person from what he could tell, but that didn't mean he wanted to marry and spend the rest of his life with her.

It would do no good to tell *Dawdi* that he wasn't angry with *Gott*, because he was. Very angry. Yes, he loved the Lord with all his heart, but why had He taken Susan and *Daed* away when the *familye* still needed them so badly?

Dawdi leaned against the doorway. "Your *vadder* was wrong to bring Abby here without your approval, but I believe he had your best interests in mind. No doubt he intended to speak with you about it, but he never got the chance. I hope you won't feel too harshly toward him."

Jakob didn't respond, wishing they could talk about something else. He had loved and respected his father, but he had no idea what the man's intentions had been. Jakob was no longer a young lad. He was a grown man with *kinder* of his own, and he had earned the right to choose whom he did and did not marry. His father had been out of line to make promises of marriage to Abby without asking him about it first.

"What are you going to do about Abby?" *Dawdi* pressed.

Jakob resisted the urge to look up from his milking. "Nothing. We will let her work and live here as long as she wants. I'm not inclined to send her back to her *familye* if she doesn't want to go."

He told his grandfather about his altercation with Simon all those years ago when they had been teenage boys. He didn't want to send her back to a life of abuse.

Dawdi grunted. "Her *daed* was no better. I knew him well when we still lived in Ohio. A cruel man, for sure. Everyone in the district knew he beat his horses, wife and kids. Some even believe he was responsible for his wife's death. His abuse was a constant point of contention in his home. The bishop and deacon spoke to him about it many times, but he never changed. The Lord taught us that loving persuasion is the way for us to lead our households. Otherwise, your *familye* learns to hate and fear you. And that's not the way for any man to be."

"I agree with you," Jakob said.

Many Amish spanked their *kinder*, but not Jakob. No matter how disobedient, he could never bring himself to beat his wife or children if they chose not to do as he asked. They were too precious to him, and he didn't want to become their enemy. But Reuben was getting out of control. Maybe a spanking was what he needed right now.

Dawdi made a *tsking* sound. "*Ach*, it's just as well that it didn't work out between you and Abby. But no matter. One of the other young men in our district will surely want to marry her. She's beautiful, young and filled with faith. I doubt she'll be living with us for very long."

With those words, *Dawdi* picked up his bucket and carried it outside, leaving Jakob alone with his thoughts. Jakob stared after the man, stunned by what his grandfather had said.

The thought of another man paying attention to Abby bothered him for some odd reason. They wouldn't know about the abuse she'd suffered. Even Jakob sensed that he didn't know all the facts. She needed a man who was patient, kind and compassionate. Someone who would adore her and never raise a hand to her or their children.

He tried to tell himself it wasn't his business. Abby could marry whomever she liked. It wasn't his place to interfere. And yet, he felt responsible for her now, especially since she had come here with plans to wed him and was now living in his household. And for the first time since she'd arrived, he actually felt bad that he couldn't give her what she desired.

Abby was just preparing to go upstairs when Jakob brought the children inside for bed. They kissed their grandmother, then trolleyed off to brush their teeth with their father's supervision. Hiding a yawn, Abby soon followed. Standing on the landing, she peered into the room the children shared. Two twin beds sat apart from each other, budged up against opposite walls. Curious about the kids' relationship with their father, Abby listened for a moment.

"Will you read us a story, *Daed*?" Reuben asked, holding up a children's book.

"Of course." Jakob took the book and sprawled across the boy's bed, his long legs hanging over the edge.

He plumped the pillows as Ruby joined them, wearing a simple flannel nightgown. She cuddled against her father and laid her head back. Abby plastered herself against the outside wall so they wouldn't see her, but she couldn't bring herself to leave. Not once in her life could she remember her father reading her a bedtime story, and she was captivated by the event.

Jakob read a tale about an Amish girl named Lily and her adventures around the farm. He brought the story to life, using a different voice for each character. When his tone lowered to a deep bass as he read the grandfather's lines, Abby had to stifle a laugh. Soon, the story ended and Jakob urged the kids to sleep.

Abby peeked around the corner. With the children lying in their separate beds, Jakob snuggled the blankets around each of their chins, then kissed them both on the forehead. She had no doubt he loved his children with all his might. In fact, his show of affection told her that he hadn't spanked Reuben earlier. If he had, the boy would still be angry and pull away. Wouldn't he?

"I miss *Mammi*," Reuben said.

"Me, too," Ruby responded.

"I know. But she's with *Gott* now. She's also still here with us, in our hearts. She'll never leave us," Jakob said.

"How can she be with *Gott* and be in our hearts, too?" Ruby asked, her forehead furrowing.

"Because we remember her. If we think of her often and know what she would want us to say and do, she can be with us always. By that way, she lives in our hearts," Jakob said.

"Truly?" Ruby whispered.

"Truly," Jakob returned. "But you must be kind to Abby. It's not her fault that *Mamm* died. And Abby has her own sadness to deal with, too."

"Like what?" Reuben asked in a challenging voice.

"Both of her parents are gone and she's all alone in the world. Life has not been easy for her."

"Really? She doesn't even have a *familye*?" Ruby's voice sounded so sad.

"Not anymore," Jakob said. "Just a *bruder* who never treated her well. She came here looking for a *familye* of her own."

"*Ach*, she can't have mine. She should go back to Ohio." Reuben's tone was heavy with resentment.

"She's not trying to take any of us away from

you, Reuben. She just needs a place to stay. We talked about this, and you will treat Abby with respect. You will treat your *schweschder* better, too. Understood?"

Abby was glad that Jakob told the boy to treat his sister well. But the boy made no verbal reply, and Abby wondered if he had nodded or merely refused to comply.

"Gutte' nacht," Jakob said.

"Ich liebe dich, Daedi," Ruby called.

"I love you, too, *boppli*," Jakob said.

He turned to leave and Abby darted into her room and carefully shut the door. She didn't want to be caught eavesdropping, and yet she was fascinated by Jakob Fisher and his *kinder*.

I love you.

The simple words of an innocent child to her father. How Abby longed to hear those words directed at her, but she knew now that it would never be. Other than her mother, no one had ever loved her, except *Gott*. And as long as she had the Lord on her side, she had faith that all would be well for her. She couldn't blame Reuben for feeling threatened and wanting to protect his mother's memory. He was just a young child who missed his mom. And once again, she envied Jakob and his loving, wonderful *familye*.

Chapter Three

Starlight gleamed through the windows in the *dawdy haus*. The cloying scent of the spearmint ointment *Dawdi* used on his arthritic joints lingered in the air. Jakob blinked his eyes, gritty with fatigue, and wished he could sleep. After a restless night, he'd finally dozed off and then awoken two hours early. He couldn't stop thinking about his father and how he'd arranged to bring Abby Miller to their farm under false pretenses. Nor could he stop worrying about Reuben, or the farm, or his mother, or a million other concerns. He needed to trust the Lord more, but lately his faith had wavered.

Staring into the darkness, Jakob lay on the small twin-size bed inside his grandfather's room. It had been his grandmother's bed before she'd died five years earlier. He listened to *Dawdi's* low, even snores and remembered a time when he'd been content enough to sleep through the night. Now, he was too troubled to rest more than an hour or two. His racing mind wouldn't settle down. After several years of drought, they had finally enjoyed a wet winter. They'd made it through the lean times, but they were short on funds and he was eager to get the fields planted so they could sell their crops. Once they delivered the hutch he'd recently finished, the payment would also help.

Sitting up, he tossed the quilt aside and padded across the wood floor in bare feet. In the tiny bathroom, he closed the door before lighting a kerosene lamp. He quickly washed and shaved his upper lip so that no moustache would accompany his tidy beard. Turning the lamp down low, he emerged from the bathroom and dressed in the dark, his grandfather's snores undisturbed by his movements. Walking outside, he closed the front door quietly behind him and stood on the porch for a moment.

Joe, their black-and-white dog, greeted him. His pink tongue lolled out of his mouth.

"*Hallo*, boy." Jakob patted the animal's head.

The chill morning air embraced him, and he took several deep breaths. Moonlight sprayed across the graveled driveway. His gaze swept over the open fields where their cattle grazed peacefully. A small stream ran past their place, swollen with spring runoff. He should speak with Reuben and Ruby about staying away from the swirling water where it deepened near the irrigation ditch…it could be dangerous to a young child. Thankfully, they should have enough water for their crops this year. Since his father brought his *familye* to Colorado ten years earlier, they had worked hard to build their farm into a prosperous place to live. Although they earned only half their living off the farm and the rest from the bakery and furniture he sold, Jakob loved it here and hoped to one day pass this land on to his children. Hope for a better future was the main reason his father had brought them here in the first place.

He held the lamp high as he walked to the barn. Joe trotted happily beside him, his stumpy tail wagging. Opening the heavy door, Jakob caught the warm earthy smell of dust, animals and straw.

"Abby!"

She stood in front of the grain bin, fully dressed and holding a silver pail and scoop of chicken feed. Another lamp had been lit and hung on a hook beside her head. The warm glow illuminated her lavender dress, white apron and *kapp*, making her look small and fragile among the shadows. Her eyes widened with momentary surprise, then she smiled and brushed a hand across her long skirts in a gesture that told him she was suddenly nervous.

"*Guder mariye*, Jakob."

"Good morning," he returned.

He closed the barn door to shut out the chilly air, then walked to her. "Why are you up so early?"

She took two steps back, not quite meeting his eyes. "I couldn't sleep, so I thought I'd make myself useful. I suspect I'm used to getting up two hours earlier in Ohio." She glanced at him. "Why are you up so early?"

He shrugged. "The same reason. I couldn't sleep either, although Ohio has nothing to do with it."

She laughed, her blue eyes twinkling and her face lighting up. In the lamp glow, she was absolutely stunning and he couldn't take his eyes off her. He realized she had as many worries on her mind as he did. And for some reason, he wished he could ease her fears and bring her a bit of comfort.

"It appears we both suffer from insomnia," she said.

"I guess so." He couldn't help returning her smile.

Stepping closer, he reached up to remove a piece of straw from her *kapp*. She jerked back and lifted both hands, as if to protect herself.

In the process, she dropped the pail and scoop. Chicken feed spattered across the barn floor. Her breathing quickened, her eyes wide and wary, as if she expected him to strike her.

Jakob drew back in surprise. He held perfectly still, waiting for her to relax. Then he plucked the piece of straw and held it out to her.

"I meant you no harm." He spoke gently, trying to soften the tense mood. But in his heart, he couldn't help wondering at her actions.

"Danke." She stooped over and swept up the spilled feed with her hands, funneling it into the pail.

He noticed that she never turned her back on him, but positioned herself so she could always see him. Something told him it was a protective instinct she'd learned from living with her father and brother, and he couldn't help wondering if they had a tendency to ambush her when she wasn't looking.

When he crouched down to help her, she drew away again, her entire body stiff. And then he knew. Simon and her father's abuse had been worse than he first thought. This gentle, soft-spoken woman was afraid of men.

She was afraid of him.

"I'll never hurt you, Abby. You are safe here. This I vow," he said.

She met his gaze, her lips slightly parted.

Her eyes filled with doubt, and he wasn't sure she believed him.

She stood abruptly and gave a nervous laugh. "I had better get the chickens fed. Do you want me to turn them out into the yard, or leave them in the coop?"

"*Ja*, turn them out. The dog will not bother them, and *Dawdi* will be here to watch over the place while we go into town."

"Unless you object, I'll feed the pigs also," she said.

He nodded and she hurried to the door, but paused there to look over her shoulder at him. "Are…are we taking the children with us into town?"

Her voice carried a bit of hesitancy, and he didn't need to ask why. No doubt she was still wary of Reuben and wished to avoid the boy.

"*Ja*, but we'll be dropping Reuben off at school. Ruby will spend the day with you and *Mamm*."

"*Gut*. I want to spend more time getting to know Reuben, so that he realizes I mean him no harm. I hope we can one day be friends."

Once again, she surprised him. She didn't want to avoid the boy. Instead, she sought the opportunity to be near him. Not what Jakob expected at all.

She stepped outside and closed the barn door.

He felt the urge to go after her. To apologize once more for frightening her. To make her laugh again. But he knew that would be a mistake. It might make her think he had changed his mind and wanted to marry her after all. That there could be something between them. And there couldn't. Not ever.

"Reuben, get your coat. We're going to be late," Naomi called to the boy from the stairs. Her arms were laden with a shallow box of freshly wrapped blueberry muffins.

The boy's bare feet thudded against the stairs as he ran down them and hurried into the kitchen. He thrust his arms into his plain black sack coat. "Where's my lunch?"

"Here it is." Abby turned from the counter, holding a red personal-sized lunch cooler.

He came to a screeching halt. "Did...did you make my lunch?"

She nodded and smiled, handing the cooler to him. "*Ja*, and I put something extra special inside. I hope you like it."

He scowled at her but took the handle, careful to avoid touching her hand. As he studied the box, she could tell he wanted to stop right there and open the lid to view the contents, but Naomi called to him again.

"Reuben! *Koom* on."

The boy turned and ran outside. Picking up a box that contained six loaves of carefully wrapped homemade bread, Abby followed. On the porch, she set the box down on a table and closed the front door securely behind her.

"I'll see you all later," *Dawdi* Zeke called from near the workshop.

"Vaarwel." Abby waved as she picked up the box of bread and stepped down off the porch.

Jakob had already pulled the buggy wagon up in front of the house. The back of the wagon was filled with carefully packed breads, rolls, cupcakes, cookies and pies for the bakery. He hopped out of the buggy to help her put the box in the back. As he did so, his hand brushed against hers and she jerked back, the warm feel of his skin zinging up her arm.

Looking up, she noticed that Naomi had managed to climb in the back of the buggy with Reuben and Ruby. That meant Abby would have to ride in the front with Jakob.

He helped her into the buggy, then hurried around to the driver's seat. Taking the leads in his strong hands, he released the brake and slapped the leather gently against the horse's back.

"Schritt."

The horse stepped forward in a steady walk. In the close quarters, Abby gazed out her open window, conscious of Jakob's knee brushing against her skirts from time to time.

When they reached the county road leading into Riverton, Jakob directed the horse over to the far right side of the road. Several cars and a truck whizzed past, and Abby was relieved when they took a turn onto another dirt road. Within fifteen minutes, they passed wide-open fields and an apple orchard.

"The Beilers live down there." Naomi pointed. "We buy our apples from them. You'll meet Lizzie at the bakery. She makes the best pies in the district."

"Not better than yours, *Grossmammi*," Reuben said.

"That's because I use her crust recipe. It's so tender and flaky. She's a very *gut* cook." Naomi smiled.

It wouldn't be appropriate for the woman to brag, but Abby could tell her grandson's words had pleased her.

Abby saw the schoolhouse long before they reached it. A white frame building with a small bell tower sat amid a fenced-off yard in the middle of a hay field. Two outhouses sat in one isolated corner. A teeter-totter and baseball diamond were the only play equipment in the yard.

The horse pulled the buggy wagon down the lane, and Jakob stopped them just out front of the schoolhouse. Several boys dressed in similar clothes waved at Reuben.

"Mach's gut." The boy bid farewell, then hopped out and ran toward them in bare feet.

"Wait! Your lunch," Abby called.

The boy stopped. Turned. With a huff, he walked back to the wagon. Abby picked up his forgotten cooler and handed it to him with a smile.

"Have a *gut* day," she said.

Under the heavy stare of his father, Reuben gave a slight nod, then turned and raced over to his friends.

Jakob made a clicking noise and the horse walked on. They passed another buggy coming into the schoolyard. They waved, but Jakob didn't stop to chat. Abby could see the woman craning her neck to look at her and was grateful he kept going. She would have plenty of people to meet and questions to answer at church on Sunday.

"Reuben said you put something special in his lunch box," Ruby said.

Abby turned in her seat, conscious of Jakob's interest in the conversation. *"Ja,* that's true."

"Is it a real nice surprise?" Ruby asked, obviously digging for more information.

"I think so. Would you like to know what it is?"

The girl nodded eagerly, a wisp of brown hair escaping her small *kapp*.

Reaching into her purse, Abby withdrew a carefully wrapped bag of chocolate chip cookies tied with a bit of yellow string. While Naomi made breakfast, she'd prepared them for the bakery.

"I was saving the cookies to give to you later on, but if it's okay with your *vadder*, you can have them now," she said.

Ruby leaned forward and pressed her cheek against her father's shoulder. "May I have them now? Please, *Daedi*?"

Abby's heart melted. The girl asked so sweetly that it would be difficult for anyone to refuse her anything.

Jakob chuckled. "*Ja*, you may."

Abby handed the cookies over.

"*Danke.*" The girl undid the string and then made an exclamation of surprise. "*Ach*, what is this?" she asked, holding up a little slip of paper with writing on it.

"What does it say? Can you read it?" Abby asked, knowing very well what it said since she had written the note.

Ruby tried to sound out the words, but got only the first three correct.

""You have an amazing smile."" Naomi read it out loud for her.

"I do?" Ruby asked.

"You most certainly do," Jakob said from the front seat.

"*Ja*, you do." Abby faced forward and hid a satisfied smile. She'd written something similar on a piece of paper for Reuben, too. Simple words that would hopefully make him smile.

"That's nice," Naomi said.

The girl showed the paper to her father. "See what Abby gave me, *Daed*?"

Jakob nodded, looking at Abby with a thoughtful frown. "*Ja*, it was very nice of her."

"I hope it makes you feel *gut*," Abby said, thinking that Ruby and Reuben needed to hear something positive for a change. Maybe her notes would help them feel not quite so lonely for their mother.

"When I go to school, I'll learn to read better." Ruby tucked the note into her hand, obviously planning to keep it.

"You'll learn many interesting things in school," Abby agreed, remembering her own education as some of the fondest times in her life. For those few hours each day, she had been free of her father and brother. Free to be herself. Free to be happy.

After eighth grade, she'd had to return to the house, where she'd been constantly at their mercy. When her father had died three years earlier, she'd had no choice but to live with her brother and his new wife.

"The Hostetlers live down that road. They raise nothing but hay and draft horses. They sell their Percherons to buyers all across the nation. They hire big trucks to come in and transport the hay for them," Naomi said.

She pointed out several other points of interest as they rode the rest of the way into town. Ruby munched on her cookies, even sharing one with her father. By the time they arrived in the alleyway behind the bakery on Main Street, they were in fairly good spirits.

"Guder mariye!" Sarah Yoder greeted them as Jakob pulled the buggy wagon to a stop and hopped out. Two other buggies were parked in the alleyway with men and women carrying baked goods into the store.

"How are you?" Naomi asked Sarah as she helped Ruby climb down from the buggy.

"Gut." Sarah smiled at Abby. "You look much more rested than when we first met yesterday."

"I am, *danke.*"

"Let me help you." The woman took the box of frosted cupcakes Abby had lifted out of the back of the wagon, leaving her free to retrieve something else.

"Danke." Abby smiled.

As they walked into the store, Sarah leaned closer and spoke low so that other people wouldn't overhear. "Have you decided to stay in Riverton after all?"

Abby nodded. "For the time being."

Sarah's gaze followed Jakob as he carried a heavy case of baked goods into the store. "Amos and I both hope you might soon find a reason to stay permanently."

Abby understood the woman's meaning perfectly, but didn't acknowledge it. She didn't want gossip to spread that she and Jakob were courting. Because they weren't.

Inside the shop, Abby helped fill the display cases with fragrant pastries, pies, breads and other baked goods. Ruby helped, too, picking up each wrapped loaf of bread carefully before handing it over to Abby.

"You're new to the district, aren't you?"

Abby looked up from her work. An attractive young woman with reddish-blond hair and wearing a sky-blue dress and white apron stood next to her, arranging a tray of frosted sugar cookies.

"*Ja*, I'm from Ohio."

"I'm Lizzie Beiler. My *familye* is from Lancaster County. We moved here eight years ago."

"I'm Abby. Abby Miller," she said.

Lizzie nodded, but her slight smile didn't

quite reach her eyes and it quickly faded. "I'm glad to meet you, Abby. Are you going to be working here in the bakery now?"

Abby shook her head. "*Ne*, do you work here?"

"*Ne*, Sarah has two older daughters who help her run the place, but one of them will be marrying soon. Since you're new in town, I thought perhaps Sarah might have hired you."

"I'm just helping Naomi drop off her baked goods."

Lizzie slid the tray of cookies into the display case. "The store is only open two days a week, on Fridays and Saturdays. In a town this size, there isn't enough business to keep it open more often than that. Everyone knows the hours and they come in to buy their bread, pies and cookies for the week. A number of us make baked goods to sell. We use the same recipes for consistency. Sarah usually sells everything by close of business on Saturday evening."

"Ah, I see."

"Abby, we're ready to go," Naomi called to her from the doorway, wiping her hands on her long apron.

Ruby ran to her grandmother. Jakob stood just behind Naomi, speaking to Bishop Amos Yoder. He shifted his weight, seeming a bit nervous. He glanced at Abby, and she wondered what the two men were discussing. When Jakob nodded and turned away, she breathed in silent relief. No doubt he was eager to get their shopping done so he could return home to his work there.

"Goodbye," Abby said.

Lizzie waved farewell, but she still didn't smile.

Abby joined Naomi and stepped outside into the morning sunshine.

"I see you've met Lizzie," Naomi said.

"*Ja*, she was nice and friendly, but she seemed kind of sad." Her gaze drifted to the doorway where Lizzie had stepped outside with her empty basket. The young woman looked up, shading her eyes against the sun.

"That's because she's still missing Eli," Naomi said.

"Eli?"

"Eli Stoltzfus, her fiancé. He left a couple of years ago… I lose track of time. They were supposed to get married, but he wanted to go to college. The night before they were to be baptized together, he abandoned our faith and joined the *Englisch* in Denver. He didn't even have the common courtesy to say goodbye or write Lizzie a note. Nothing. He just left."

"Oh, how sad," Abby said, understanding how that must have hurt his *familye* and Lizzie.

"I understand from his *mudder* that he is doing very well in school," Naomi continued. "He hasn't even written to Lizzie. He broke her heart, and she hasn't been the same since. Now, she won't attend the singings or even think about getting married. I fear she's lost her trust in men."

Abby felt a powerful rush of sympathy. She didn't trust men either. Her heart had been broken, too, but for different reasons. Neither she nor Lizzie wanted to marry. Not after the painful betrayal they'd experienced at the hands of men they should have been able to trust.

Looking up, Abby saw Jakob leaning against the buggy, his ankles crossed. With the warmth of the day, he'd rolled the long sleeves of his shirt up to his elbows and pushed the straw hat back on his head. She blinked, thinking him the most handsome man she'd ever seen.

Ruby was already sitting quietly in the back of the buggy, a perpetual smile on her face.

Beneath the brim of his hat, Jakob watched his mother and Abby. From his calm exterior, he appeared to be patiently waiting for them. But Abby sensed a nervous energy in him. No doubt he was eager to return home.

"We better go. I don't want to keep Jakob waiting any longer," Naomi said.

Abby agreed. She hurried past Naomi and

climbed into the back of the buggy with Ruby. Ever considerate, Jakob reached to help her, but she pretended not to notice and quickly sat beside the little girl. Ruby leaned against her. Unable to resist the girl's open affection, Abby lifted her arm around her slender shoulders and cuddled the child close to her side.

Jakob helped his mother. Naomi gave him a sweet smile and patted his arm. When she sat back, Abby heard her breathing heavily, as though she couldn't catch her breath. It had been a hectic morning. No doubt the woman needed a rest from her busy day.

Jakob rounded the buggy to climb into the driver's seat, then took the leads and clicked his tongue. As the horse moved into a quick trot down the street, Abby wished that things could be different somehow. But Jakob loved his wife. He didn't want her. And longing for something that could never be would only bring more discontent to Abby's heart.

Chapter Four

That afternoon, Abby carried the heavy rag rug from the main living room outside to the backyard. Swinging it up, she struggled for a moment to get it draped over the strong rope line that stretched between two wooden poles. Picking up a wicker rug beater, she pounded the rug for several moments. Clouds of dust wafted into the air. Bright sunlight streamed across the yard, highlighting the flower beds where yellow tulips and daffodils were just starting to bloom.

Thirty minutes. That's how long she had before she'd need to pull two cherry pies out of the oven. She'd set the timer on the front porch, so she'd be sure to hear it when it rang. Just enough time to get some house cleaning done.

Ruby was inside with Naomi, helping dust the furniture. To ease Naomi's workload, Abby had insisted on mopping the wooden floors herself. Soon, Reuben would be home from school. She was eager to hear his comments over the special note she'd tucked into his cookie bag. Hopefully the message had made him happy.

Tugging on the rug, she adjusted its position and smacked it several times in different places. She coughed and waved a hand in the air to disperse the dust. The sound of horses drew her attention, and she faced the south pasture. On the opposite side of the barbed wire fence, Jakob sat on a disc plow with a two-team hitch. The moment she saw him, a buzz of excitement pulsed through her body. She didn't understand why, but her senses went on high alert every time he was near.

The two gigantic draft horses pulled the plow with ease. Jakob held the lead lines in his strong hands, his body swaying gently as the blades sliced through the heavy clods of dirt. His straw hat was pulled low over his eyes, casting his face in shadow. He didn't look up as he passed, his focus directed at the dappled Percherons as they plowed in long, even furrows. Abby was amazed that anyone could handle such big horses, but she knew they were nothing more than gentle giants. She had been here only one day and already couldn't help admiring Jakob's strength and hard work ethic. In spite of taking them to the bakery in town that morning, he had plowed half of the fields. Neither her father nor Simon had ever been so industrious, and she couldn't help making numerous comparisons.

As he reached the end of the row and turned the horses, Jakob lifted his head and looked straight at her. Feeling suddenly self-conscious, Abby tugged the rug off the rope line and hurried toward the house. When she returned fifteen minutes later with the rug from the kitchen, Jakob and the horses were nowhere to be seen. She had just enough time to clean this rug before her pies needed to come out of the oven.

"Abby!"

She turned. Wearing a blue work apron over his clothes, *Dawdi* Zeke stood in front of the workshop. He beckoned to her, and she tossed her wicker stick onto the lawn. As she walked toward him, she brushed dust off her long skirts.

"I just finished staining the china hutch. Would you like to see it?" he asked when she drew near.

Abby glanced back at the house, thinking about her pies. She nodded, returning his exuberant smile. "*Ja*, but I only have a few minutes."

"That's time enough." He turned and hobbled into the workshop.

Filled with curiosity, she followed. On the outside, the building appeared to be nothing more than a detached three-car garage the men had built themselves. From references made at supper last night, she knew this was where they made furniture. In addition to the farm and bakery, this was undoubtedly a side business that brought extra income to the *familye*.

As Abby stepped inside, bright overhead lights powered by a gas generator made it easy to see. The air smelled of sawdust and varnish. Along one wall, tall metal shelves were lined with tidy stacks of lumber. The bare cement floors were well swept. A wide broom leaned against the open door along with several garbage cans filled with wood shavings and sawdust.

"We use the shavings as kindling for our fires and nesting material for the chickens. Nothing goes to waste," Zeke said.

Along the far wall, several rocking chairs, oak benches, tables and a chest of drawers were in various stages of completion. At the back of the room, a huge bench stood with plenty of room to work on their projects. Along the entire width of the wall, hooks had been affixed to a fiberboard and held an assortment of clamps, screwdrivers, chisels, drills, hammers, levels, saws, tape measures and other items all hanging in their place. Abby wasn't surprised by the orderliness of the shop. She was fast learning that this *familye* took special care with every facet of their life.

Sitting next to the workbench was an ornate buffet and china hutch. A sparkling mirror had been set into the back of the hutch. No doubt it would highlight any dishes that were put inside on the shelves. The rich brown stain of the wood accented the embellished pilasters and complex detailing of the appliqués. Abby tried not to be impressed by its opulent beauty, but she honestly couldn't help it. She would never own such decorative furniture. It was much too exquisite for a plain Amish home. Too prideful. But she couldn't help admiring the skill that had made the piece.

"What do you think?" *Dawdi* Zeke asked.

"It's…it's nice," she said, trying to find the right words that wouldn't sound too prideful.

"*Dawdi*, I need to sharpen the blades on the plow again. There are too many rocks in that farthest field…" Jakob pulled up short as he entered the shop and saw Abby standing there with Zeke.

Dawdi Zeke turned. "I can help with that. I've finished my work. Does it look all right?"

The older man gestured to the hutch. As Jakob walked over to them, Abby felt the weight of his gaze resting on her. She met his eyes briefly, then they all stared at the hutch. Jakob circled the grand piece of oak, surveying it with a critical eye. Finally, he nodded with approval. "It looks fine. You did a *gut* job covering up all the flaws in the wood. What do you think, Abby?"

The two men looked at her, waiting expectantly for her verdict.

She schooled her features so she wouldn't overly express her awe. "*Ja*, it's fine."

What an understatement. The piece was absolutely beautiful, but she refused to say so. It wouldn't be appropriate. She could hardly believe that a man of Zeke's advanced years and with his trembly hands could do such delicate work.

"*Gut*. Jason Crawley commissioned it for his wife. It's their fortieth wedding anniversary next week. I was worried we wouldn't have it ready in time," Jakob said.

"I've just put on the last coat of stain. We can deliver it to Jason on Tuesday or Wednesday, after you've finished the planting," *Dawdi* Zeke said.

Abby looked at Zeke. "I'm sure Mr. Crawley will be very satisfied with your work."

Dawdi Zeke snorted, resting one gnarled hand on his hip. "All I did was stain the wood. Jakob did all the work. He makes all our furniture now that my hands are so shaky."

Which meant that Jakob had made the furniture in her bedroom, too. And once again, she felt a tad guilty for chasing him out of his room, but was touched by his generosity.

"I stain everything because it's easy work and I need something useful to do. I'm old and not much good at anything else," *Dawdi* Zeke said.

"That's not true. You taught me everything I know and you have an excellent eye for staining. I couldn't do it without you," Jakob said.

Zeke chuckled. "*Ja*, but I've never had your feel for the wood grain. You seem to know just how to cut the wood."

Abby looked at Jakob, impressed by the respect he showed his grandfather. She had thought Zeke built the furniture. "I didn't know you both were carpenters."

"*Ja*, we built the house and barn ourselves. Of course, *Daed* was alive back then and helped," Jakob said in a matter-of-fact voice. "But furniture making is just a sideline we do in our free time. *Dawdi* and my *vadder* taught me. It brings in some extra funds."

Free time? She hadn't been here long, but

hadn't noticed any of them ever sitting idle. There always seemed work to do. It had been the same back home in Ohio.

"Someday, Jakob would like to open a furniture shop in town, but he's afraid we wouldn't get enough business for us to earn a living full-time," *Dawdi* Zeke said.

"You won't know unless you try," she said.

Jakob nodded, his ears slightly red with modesty. "We'll see. Maybe in another year. Word will get out and I'll have more customers. I don't want to jeopardize our livelihood until we are sure we can make it through a lean spell. Time will tell."

Yes, time would tell a lot of things. Right now, she had no idea where she might be this time next year. But she knew one thing for certain. If not for the deaths of Jakob's wife and father, Abby believed these people would be very happy. And she couldn't help wishing she could be a permanent part of their *familye*.

"Abby! Your pies are all burnt up."

Abby gasped and whirled toward the door. Jakob turned and saw Ruby standing there breathing hard, as if she'd run all the way from the house.

"Oh, no! I got caught up in our conversa-

tion and forgot all about them." Picking up her
skirts, Abby ran outside.

Jakob followed, just in case there was a fire
he needed to help put out.

As they approached the back door, billows
of thick smoke wafted from the kitchen. Jakob
stood back as Naomi pulled the smoking rem-
nants of the blackened pies out of the oven and
scurried outside to set them far away from the
house. Jakob grabbed the fire extinguisher they
kept hanging on the wall in the laundry room,
but there was no need. The fire was out and the
pies were ruined.

"Oh, I'm so sorry. I lost track of time and let
them burn." Abby quickly opened all the windows and propped the door wide, waving her
arms to get the smoke to filter outside.

"You should have paid more attention. Now
we won't have pie for supper," Reuben said.

The boy stood beside Ruby in the doorway
leading to the living room, having just gotten
home from school after Naomi went to fetch
him in the buggy. In Ohio, the schoolhouse was
close enough that the children could walk to
school. But here in Riverton, their farms were
spread too far apart.

A disapproving scowl creased Reuben's forehead. Abby glanced at him, then ducked her
head. But not before Jakob saw the absolute

misery in her eyes. Her face was flushed red from the heat of the kitchen or embarrassment, Jakob wasn't sure which. Probably both.

"I'm… I'm truly sorry," she said again. "I can fix it. I'll go right to work and make new pies. I can have them ready by suppertime."

She hurried over to the cupboard and pulled out a mixing bowl and canister of flour. Not only did she seem jittery, but also frightened. As though there might be horrible repercussions for her failing to watch the pies more carefully.

"There's no need for that. We've got other things to do now. Heaven knows I've burned my share of pies and numerous other dishes in this kitchen, too." Naomi bustled back into the house and took hold of Abby's arm to stop her. With a flip of her wrist, she turned off the oven heat.

Although Jakob couldn't remember his mother ever burning a single thing, he appreciated her kind heart and cheerful support.

Abby stood back and twined her fingers together in a nervous gesture, her eyes filled with uncertainty. She wouldn't look at any of them, staring at the floor instead.

"We don't need pie tonight. Do we, Reuben?" Jakob gave his son a pointed look. They all could see that Abby felt bad enough already.

She didn't need a seven-year-old boy to act like a spoiled brat right now.

Reuben hesitated, his face twisted in an ugly glare.

"Do we, Reuben?" Jakob said again, his tone more insistent.

The child heaved a disgruntled sigh. "I guess not."

"We'll have cookies instead. I've always got tons of those on hand," Naomi said in a pleasant voice.

Reuben grimaced, as though the thought of eating a cookie sounded repulsive to him.

"I love cookies, especially chocolate chip. You can make pie tomorrow," Ruby suggested. The girl walked over to Abby and took her hand in a show of support.

"That's right. You can make pie tomorrow." Jakob smiled with encouragement, hoping to put Abby at ease. He hated that Reuben had made her feel bad. And that's when it occurred to him that she expected them to bawl her out for her mistake. Was that what Simon would have done? And would he have beaten Abby, too? The thought of anyone striking this gentle woman upset Jakob more than he could say.

"Bah! It's just pie. No use getting upset about it." *Dawdi* Zeke waved a hand from the back door, as though brushing it all away.

"Danke," Abby said, her voice a low whisper as she showed a half smile.

With the pies out of the kitchen, the black smoke soon cleared, but the stench remained. Two hours later, they finished their evening chores and gathered for supper. Night was coming on, the air brisk and cool, but Naomi kept the windows open. After prayer, Abby helped serve the meal, setting a bowl of boiled potatoes on the table.

"Abby put a special note in my cookie bag today," Ruby told Reuben.

The boy grunted as he took a huge bite of bread spread with butter and strawberry preserves.

"She put a special note in your lunch box, too. What did it say?" Ruby asked.

Everyone turned to look at Reuben. Abby's eyes glowed with anticipation.

Reuben shrugged, not looking up. "I didn't find any note in my lunch. I don't know what you're talking about."

"You didn't? What happened to it?" Ruby asked.

"I don't know. Leave me alone." The boy gave her a sharp jab with his elbow.

"Ow!"

"Reuben, be kind to your sister," Jakob said.

Abby exhaled a low sigh and blinked in bemusement. She didn't say anything, but Jakob knew she was confused. He had no doubt that she'd included an uplifting message in Reuben's lunch box, similar to the one she had written for Ruby. So what had happened to the note?

"Maybe the slip of paper fell out and was lost when you unwrapped your cookies," *Dawdi* Zeke suggested. The elderly man eased himself into his chair and rested his gnarled hands in his lap.

Jakob glanced at Abby. She was watching *Dawdi*, her eyebrows drawn together with concern. She seemed highly observant and undoubtedly noticed that *Dawdi* was in pain. She nodded at Jakob's comment and took her seat before reaching for a thick slice of bread to butter.

"I said I didn't find a note and I didn't," Reuben insisted. A deep scowl pulled his eyebrows together. He hunkered over his plate and ate in brooding silence.

Jakob sensed his son was telling a fib. He didn't like this open hostility toward Abby, but didn't feel that he could call the boy a liar without proof. Abby hadn't done anything to the child, except try to make him happy. And yet, Jakob had no idea how to get Reuben to stop being so angry at everyone. It wasn't Ruby's or Abby's fault that Susan had died. But Abby was a constant reminder of all that they'd recently lost. A reminder that they'd been happy once. And Jakob didn't understand why her presence impacted Reuben this way. But he did know one thing. He had to do something about it, before the boy grew up to be as heartless and cruel as Simon had become.

Abby closed the door to her bedroom. After cleaning up the kitchen, she'd come upstairs without a light. Standing in the dark, she breathed a sigh of relief. Now that she was alone for the night, she could finally let down her guard. She'd been so eager to win everyone's approval. Writing special notes for the children. Helping with the house chores. Making pies for supper. Trying to win their friendship. She'd failed miserably. Instead of easing Naomi's load, she'd increased the work. No matter how clean the house was, the stench of burned food permeated every room. Maybe tomorrow, she'd ask Naomi if she could wash the curtains. That might help. But what had happened to the special message she'd put in Reuben's lunch for him to find? Maybe Zeke was right and the note had fallen out when Reuben had ripped open his bag of cookies. She'd be sure to make up for it by writing him another note for his lunch box on Monday.

For now, she was exhausted, both mentally and physically. Removing her *kapp*, she laid it on the dresser, then sat on a corner of the bed and brushed out her long hair. She stifled a huge yawn as she stood, pulled the covers back and slid her legs between the sheets. She immediately scrambled out. Something prickly had dug into her feet and calves.

Her heart pounded in her chest as she considered what it might be. Spiders? Frogs? Something else creepy? She shuddered at the thought.

Using moonlight from the window so she could see, she lit the kerosene lamp and brought it over to the bed. Gathering her courage, she flipped the covers over in one hurried jerk, then jumped back expecting some kind of bugs.

Cracker crumbs!

She peered closer to be sure. Yes! Someone had sprinkled cracker crumbs between her sheets. But who…?

Oh, no. She knew the answer without asking. Reuben must have paid her room a visit. The little rascal. Did he really dislike her so much? And why? She didn't understand. No, not at all.

Sudden anger billowed up inside her. Just wait until she told Jakob what the boy had done. Reuben would be very sorry.

With stiff, sharp movements, she pulled the sheets off the bed, folding them so no crumbs fell onto the floor. She'd tried to be kind to the little boy. To go out of her way to make friends with him. And look how he repaid her.

Clutching the sheets close to her chest, she picked up the lamp and stepped out on the landing. The stairs creaked beneath her bare feet, and she moved more quietly, trying not to disturb Naomi.

Who did Reuben think he was, being so rude to her all the time? She was his elder and he should treat her with respect. In the morning, she would give him a good piece of her mind. Jakob would find out what his son had done. He would deal with the child…

She paused, standing on the front porch outside. The chilly night air helped to cool her anger, and she shivered in her modest nightgown. Opening the sheets, she shook them out on the front lawn. No doubt the chickens and other birds would eat up the crumbs.

She couldn't tell Jakob what Reuben had done. If she did, he might spank the boy. She thought about Jesus Christ and what He'd suffered for her sins. He'd harmed no one, yet His own people had demanded His death. A perfect, sinless man, and yet He'd willingly gone through excruciating pain, first in the Garden of Gethsemane when He'd made the atonement, and then upon the cross when He had died. For her. For all mankind.

Gott's only begotten Son had done that which no one else could do. He'd atoned for her sins so that she might be forgiven if only she would repent. So that she could live with *Gott* again. In all His words and deeds, Christ had set the perfect example. Then how could she show any less mercy to Reuben?

Taking a deep breath, she exhaled, letting it sweep her anger away. She must follow her Savior's example and turn the other cheek.

"Abby?"

She jerked around. "Jakob! What are you doing here?"

He stood at the side of the porch, his hair tousled and his shirt disheveled, as though he'd been awakened from sleep and dressed in a hurry. "I heard a noise out here and came to see what it was. What is that you are shaking out of your sheets?"

Peering through the dark, he eyed the lawn where white speckles of cracker crumbs covered the grass.

She quickly wadded the sheets and held them close against her chest. "It's nothing. My sheets just needed some airing."

Okay, that was true enough. She didn't want

to get Reuben into any more trouble. That wouldn't be the Savior's way.

Jakob tilted his head in confusion. "It's late. You're airing your sheets at this time of night?"

"*Ja*, but I'm finished now. *Gutte' nacht*." Before he could ask any more questions, she whirled around and hurried inside the house, closing the door securely behind her.

Peeking out the window in the living room, she watched as he headed back into the darkness toward the *dawdy haus*. He raked his fingers through his hair, shaking his head in bewilderment. Good. He had no clue what was going on.

Watching him go, Abby realized how comical the situation must seem. No doubt he thought her a very odd woman indeed. She felt suddenly light of heart and had to stifle a laugh. No harm had been done. Reuben was simply a mischievous boy who had decided he didn't like her. The poor boy. He was trying so hard to push her away, which told her that he needed a friend badly right now.

One day, she might tell Jakob what had really happened this night. He'd be disappointed in Reuben, of course. But she sensed that he would also find the boy's actions funny. And she longed to share another laugh with him. To see him smile again. But for now, an idea filled her mind and she knew exactly how she should handle the situation.

Chapter Five

The following morning, Abby got up early and made breakfast for the *familye*. The tantalizing aroma of bacon helped diminish the remaining odor of burnt pies. As she set the table, she decided the smell wasn't so bad anymore.

Naomi wrapped and loaded various baked goods into large boxes for delivery at the bakery. While the muffins baked, Abby helped her.

"I'd like to remain behind today, if that's all right. I'd like to try once more to bake pies for our supper, just to show you that I can," Abby said.

"I have no doubt of your ability." Naomi patted her shoulder. "Jakob will finish the plowing today, then he and *Dawdi* will be taking the hutch into town to Mr. Crawley. Reuben doesn't have school today, but I'll take the children with me. It'll keep them busy and out of your hair for a while."

"Danke." Abby nodded in agreement, thinking this might be wise. She wanted nothing to distract her this time and planned to remain inside the house until she was finished.

"I'll do the mending while the pies bake and then prepare a stew for supper," Abby said.

"Oh, would you? That would make my day so much easier. *Ach*, I'm so glad you're here." Naomi gave her a spontaneous hug.

"It's my pleasure." Abby blinked her eyes fast to keep tears from falling. The woman's gesture touched her like nothing else could, and she wrapped her arms around her shoulders.

Ruby and Reuben entered the kitchen fully dressed and ready for their day. When Jakob joined them moments later, Abby forced herself to act casual, but her heart rate tripped into double time.

Tossing her a knowing look, Reuben slid into his chair. He wore a satisfied smirk, as though he were very pleased with himself. Knowing what he'd done, he actually seemed to welcome a fight. He glowered at her, like a cat ready to pounce on a bird.

Flipping two pancakes in the frying pan, Abby pretended not to notice as she set the serving plate in front of the two children. Con-

tention was not of *Gott*. She was not going to
fight with the boy nor say or do anything that
might cause friction between him and Jakob.
She was the adult here. She could handle this
situation well enough. She hoped.

"*Guder mariye*. Reuben, I hope you're feeling well today. And you, too, Ruby." Abby
spoke in her most cheerful voice.

"How did you sleep last night?" Reuben
asked, his voice low and sly.

"*Ach*, like a log," Abby said. "*Ja*, I had the
best night's sleep in I don't know how long.
Thank you for asking."

"You did?" Reuben asked, looking slightly
taken off guard.

"*Ja*, I did." Abby thoroughly enjoyed the look
of confusion on his face. She had no doubt he
expected her to react to what he had done to
her sheets. But she had other plans.

As the men gathered around the table, Abby
bided her time. Most of the food was on the
table, and she waited for the prayer to end, then
cleared her voice to gain everyone's attention.

"I'd like to thank all of you for your warm
hospitality to me," she said. "You've all been
so kind. Especially Reuben."

She gazed at the boy steadily, forcing herself
not to flinch as he looked up, his eyes widen-

ing. Out of her peripheral vision, she noticed Jakob's curious glance as he listened to her.

"Knowing how nervous and lonely I must be and trying to adjust to a strange place and fit in with new people, Reuben has been especially *gut* and generous to me," she continued. "He has been so considerate, going out of his way to welcome me. I especially appreciate the thoughtful gift he left for me last night. It was so hospitable of him."

Jakob stared at her with puzzlement, but *Dawdi* Zeke chuckled, seeming to understand what was going on. Surely he didn't know about the cracker crumbs, but Abby thought the older man was smart enough to figure it out.

Reuben was overly quiet, staring at his plate, his face red with guilt. For a moment, Abby thought he might burst into tears. If nothing else, she'd made him think about what he'd done. If he had a conscience—and Abby believed that he did—then he'd think twice before purposefully trying to hurt her again.

"What gift did you leave for Abby?" Naomi asked.

"*Ja*, what gift?" Ruby chimed in.

"That's between Reuben and me. Would you pass the potatoes, please?" Abby smiled sweetly as she looked at Jakob. She was determined to love his children no matter what.

Jakob handed her a bowl. "Does this have anything to do with you shaking out your bed-sheets late last night?"

Naomi jerked her head up. "What? Why were you shaking out your sheets? I washed them the day before you arrived. They should have been clean."

"They just needed a little airing," Abby said. She ducked her head and began to eat, but she caught Naomi's look of puzzlement. Thankfully, she didn't push the issue.

Everyone became overly quiet and subdued, except for *Dawdi* Zeke. The elderly man grinned from ear to ear as he filled his plate and ate with relish.

"*Ach*, I'm delighted to have you here in our home, Abby," Zeke said. "We've been in mourning too long. You're a surprising and pleasant change. You'll keep us on our toes and do us all a lot of good."

"*Danke.* I hope so," she said, trying not to blush with pleasure.

A happy, buoyant feeling settled over her. She liked how she had handled the situation with Reuben, and it gave her a small bit of confidence. But she sure wished she could somehow get the boy to stop glaring and smile for once.

After they finished their meal and dispersed

to their various activities, Abby rolled out dough and baked her cherry pies. The lattice top was a pretty golden brown.

Setting the pies aside to cool, she then prepared the noon meal. She chopped up meat and vegetables, then let them simmer in a pot. As she sat at the kitchen table, she mended a variety of socks, aprons, shirts and trousers. The rest of the day went by without incident, and at supper, everyone exclaimed over her pie. Everyone except Reuben, of course. Like always, he was sullen and quiet.

"This pie is delicious, Abby. Some of the best I've ever eaten." Zeke glanced at Reuben. "Are you sure you don't want some?"

The boy looked at the pie and fresh whipped cream with such longing that Abby thought his mouth must be watering. Maybe he would change his mind. But no. He shook his head, being stubborn.

"*Ne.* I don't like cherry pie. It's too tart."

Naomi snorted. "Since when do you not like cherry pie? And this pie is as sweet as can be. Just right."

The boy jerked his shoulders in a shrug, but Abby knew the answer. He didn't like that Abby had made the pie.

Zeke grinned. "More for us, then. But just

remember, *mein sohn*, it's not wise to cut off your nose to spite your face."

Reuben's eyebrows drew together in a questioning glance. "What does that mean, *Dawdi*?"

Zeke nodded. "You just think about it for a while. I'm sure its meaning will dawn on you sooner or later."

"*Ja*, this pie is delicious. The crust is so light and flaky. Don't you think so, Jakob?" Naomi prodded.

At that moment, the man was helping himself to a second slice, so he obviously liked it. He lifted his head, seeming startled by the question. When he looked at Abby, his features softened, but he hesitated for a moment.

"*Ja*, it's very *gut*. You did well," he finally said.

She smiled, feeling enormously relieved by his praise. Throughout her life, no one had ever thanked her or told her she'd done a nice job. Not ever. More than anything, she wanted this man's approval, and she wasn't sure why.

Jakob knew he shouldn't stay after supper. He should have gone to the *dawdy haus* instead. But honestly, he was in a good mood. He and *Dawdi* Zeke had safely delivered the hutch to Jason Crawley in town, and the payment eased some of his worries.

He sat on the couch in the living room, trying to read *The Budget* newspaper. They'd lit the kerosene lamps, and their glow provided a warm, comfy environment. Since the paper came from Ohio, it was packed with stories and news of their *familye* members and old life there. He usually enjoyed reading it to everyone, but not tonight.

His gaze kept wandering over to where Abby was laughing and chatting with his daughter. With church Sunday tomorrow, Abby had overseen Ruby's bath and was now sitting with the girl on the large rag rug in the middle of the room. She picked up a brush, preparing to comb out Ruby's long hair. Reuben now occupied the only bathroom in the house. *Dawdi* Zeke was slouched in a soft, old recliner. Naomi sat nearby, the click of her knitting needles accompanying *Dawdi's* soft snores and the ticks from the simple wooden clock on the wall. The sounds were quiet and comforting, yet Jakob felt distracted.

Sitting behind Ruby, Abby parted the girl's damp hair down the middle, then painstakingly worked each section to free the multitude of snarls.

"Your hair is very fine like mine. I want to be careful so I don't cause any breakage," Abby said.

Ruby held up a spray bottle. "My *mamm* used this for the tangles."

Abby took the bottle and kissed the girl's forehead. "Your *mamm* was very wise. Even I use detangler on my hair."

"You do?" Ruby asked, sitting perfectly still, her chin held high.

"Of course. Long hair tends to knot easily when you wash it."

Abby spritzed the child's hair, holding up one hand to shield Ruby's eyes from the spray.

"Jakob?"

He looked at his mother, who had paused in her knitting. She inclined her head toward the paper he held with both hands. "Aren't you going to read some more?"

"Oh. Sorry." He returned to reading out loud so Naomi could hear. An article about a new schoolhouse they were building in Holmes County.

Naomi paused in her knitting and raised a finger, interrupting him. "Another school? You see how crowded they're getting back east? It was wise of your *vadder* to bring us here to Colorado. Now, we have lots of room for our *familye* to grow."

Jakob nodded, having heard this statement numerous times before. Although his mother missed her own brothers, sisters and numer-

ous other *familye* members, he knew this was
~~her way of justifying her husband's decision to~~
move them west.

He finished the article, then searched for another story of interest. Ruby's laugh drew his
gaze again.

"Would you like it braided this time, or just
pulled back in a bun?" Abby asked Ruby.

"Braided, please," the girl responded with a
decisive nod of her head.

Abby picked up the long strands and began
to plait the hair, her dexterous fingers moving
quickly from front to back. Finally, she tied off
the end with a small rubber band.

"Jakob!"

He jerked, glancing over at Naomi. Seeing
her slight frown, he began to read again. In all
honesty, he had no idea what he was saying.
He couldn't seem to focus tonight and decided
he was overly tired.

"Almost finished," Abby said.

Jakob looked up as she twisted the braids
onto Ruby's head. She held bobby pins between her lips. When she was ready, she took
the pins to secure the hair, then patted the finished product with her palms. Last, but not
least, she reached for Ruby's *kapp*. Abby caught
his gaze and immediately ducked her head in
a shy but endearing glance.

"*Ach!* I can see that if I want to know what's in *The Budget*, I'll have to read the paper myself." Naomi shook her head, her lips pursed together in disgust.

Awakened by her exclamation, *Dawdi* Zeke jerked and gave a loud snort. They all laughed as he blinked his eyes open and gave a deep, yawning sigh. He had no idea that he'd been snoring and they found him so amusing.

"*Daedi*, I'm worried about Amber. She hasn't come to the house for her bowl of cream in months," Ruby said.

Jakob chuckled. "It's only been a week or two since she came around the house, not months."

"*Ach*, it seems like months. I'm worried about her."

"Who is Amber?" Abby asked.

"Our barn cat. She's expecting babies, so I've been giving her cream to help keep her healthy. But she's stopped coming around," Ruby said.

"Perhaps she had her babies," Naomi said.

Ruby gasped in alarm and looked at her father. "But who will help her if she's all alone? What will she eat?"

"Don't worry. She knows what to do and catches lots of mice to eat. She'll show up when she's good and ready. And then we'll start seeing more cats in the barn," Jakob said.

The girl showed a doubtful frown.

"It's late. I think I'll turn in." Zeke gripped the arms of his chair and stood stiffly before shuffling slowly toward the door.

"Gutte' nacht," Abby said.

"I'll be along in a few minutes," Jakob called to his grandfather's retreating back.

Dawdi waved his acknowledgment, then closed the door behind him.

"There. *Vas denkscht?*" Abby held up a small hand mirror for Ruby to view her hair.

The girl peered at herself and smiled. "I think it's *wundervoll.*"

Abby hugged the child, then gathered up the hair implements. "*Gut.* Now, it's off to bed with you."

"Ahem!"

Jakob turned and saw that Naomi had put her knitting away, having given up on his reading any more. He stood quickly.

"I'll take her upstairs," he said.

"*Ja*, it's getting late. Reuben should be finished with his bath and ready for bed, too," Naomi said.

Reaching over, Jakob snatched Ruby up and swung her high. The girl squealed with glee as he tickled her ribs and kissed her sweet-smelling neck.

Abby laughed at their gaiety and he paused,

looking at her for just a moment. Finally, he found his voice.

"Um, *danke*."

"*Ja, danke*, Abby," Ruby said.

She showed another timid smile. "You're most *willkomm*, sweetheart."

Jakob hurried toward the stairs, carrying Ruby with him. His face burned with bewilderment. For a few minutes, he'd forgotten that Abby wasn't Susan. That after he put his children to bed, he'd have to retire alone. There would be no one there to whisper with him in the darkness as they recounted the events of their day. No one to discuss the kids or planting or share ideas with or seek advice from. Abby was a constant reminder of all the joy he'd lost, and he couldn't help wishing he could regain that happiness. But Susan was gone. He had to accept that he would live the rest of his life without a wife. It would be less painful that way.

Chapter Six

As hard as Abby tried to get out the door before everyone else the following morning, she was delayed when she found her shoes filled to the brim with dirt. No doubt Reuben was responsible. She fumed for several minutes, wanting to rant and scream at the boy, but then she remembered the anger she was raised with and decided to exercise self-discipline instead.

Gripping her patience, she walked outside to the backyard in her stockinged feet. After emptying her shoes into the garden, she smacked them together to get all the little rocks out. By the time she'd tied the laces and raced out the front door, she arrived at the buggy only to discover that Zeke and Naomi were already in the backseat with the two kids. Which meant she would have to sit in the front seat with Jakob.

Again.

She glanced at Reuben, who looked down at her black sensible shoes. A sly grin flashed across his face before he turned away, looking innocent as a newborn babe.

Abby looked at *Dawdi* Zeke. Beneath the brim of his straw hat, she saw a sparkle of laughter in his gray eyes.

"There's no room in the back. You'll have to sit up front," he said.

So, he didn't know what Reuben had done. If she didn't know better, she would think he'd purposefully planned things so that she would be forced to sit next to Jakob. No doubt he'd been told her true reason for coming to Colorado. She could only assume he was match-making, but it would do no good. She and Jakob would never marry now.

Standing beside the buggy, Jakob silently took her hand and helped her up. His rough palm was warm against hers, and the slight smile he gave her only increased her nerves. She felt as though he were forcing himself to be solicitous of her. Like she was one of his chores. Although she was grateful he'd agreed to let her stay here, she didn't like being where she wasn't wanted.

She straightened her dark blue skirts, knowing she wouldn't escape notice. New members always garnered interest at church.

Jakob climbed into the buggy, released the brake and slapped the leads against the horse's back. As they pulled onto the main road, even the steady clip-clop of the horse's hooves did nothing to alleviate her worries.

Last night, she'd checked her bed and felt a small victory when she didn't find any crackers or a snake between her sheets. But now, her apprehension returned when she remembered Bishop Yoder's words.

There are not enough women of our faith to marry our young men.

She wasn't interested in being pursued by any men. The thought twisted her insides into knots. She was a stranger here and naturally shy. She didn't know what to say to young men. As an Amish woman, she knew her duty. To marry and support her husband, raising a *gut familye* in the faith. She should encourage the eligible bachelors to pay her court. To get to know them and choose one to be her life's partner. But she couldn't. Not ever. And that left her feeling rebellious, hopeless and unacceptable to *Gott*.

"Oh, *ne*. Look, *Grossmammi*. I have a hole in my dress," Ruby said.

Abby turned to look over her shoulder. Sure enough, a large section of seam had come undone in Ruby's skirt. She tugged on a long thread, then waggled her fingers through the gaping hole, showing a length of bare leg in the process.

"Oh, dear. If we return home so you can change, we'll be late for church," Naomi said, her voice sounding flustered.

"It is too late to return home," Jakob said with finality, giving a light flick of the leads for emphasis.

Naomi looked wilted. "*Ach*, Ruby can't run around like this, showing her bare legs to everyone. We'll have to turn around, Jakob."

His jaw hardened, and Abby didn't need to ask why. This wasn't Ohio where they lived close to their Amish neighbors and could soon be at church. They were far enough outside town that they had to travel eight miles one way to reach their destination. If they turned around now, they would miss most of the meetings, not to mention the fatigue on their horse.

"Don't worry. I'm sure Mrs. Stoltzfus will have a needle and thread we can borrow," Abby said. "As soon as we arrive, I'll ask if there is a private room we can go to, and I'll quickly mend the dress before our meetings start."

"Of course. Such an easy solution. I'm not thinking clearly today. *Danke*, Abby," Naomi said.

Abby reached back and squeezed the older

woman's hand. "You're just overly tired. You worked too hard to get all the cakes and breads over to the bakery yesterday. I'll help you more this next week."

Naomi gave her a smile of gratitude. "Would you mind working with Jakob on the planting tomorrow? Then I would have time to get the laundry done."

Abby felt Jakob stiffen beside her and wondered if he'd rather she stayed in the house. But she was a guest here and resigned to doing whatever they asked of her.

"Of course. I'd be happy to help." Abby smiled, but felt a flutter of unease. Helping with the planting meant she would be working most of the day with Jakob.

"But I usually drive the small wagon," Zeke said.

Naomi pursed her lips. "Not this year. You're not a young man anymore, but I'd like to keep you around as long as possible. You'll rest and help me around the house, and that's that."

Abby glanced over her shoulder and saw Zeke blink in surprise at his daughter. He didn't argue, giving in to common sense.

"Can you drive?" he asked Abby.

She lifted her chin, remembering the eight-hitch team of Belgian draft horses she'd driven numerous times in the fields for her brother.

She almost laughed, but felt no humor. And yet, a part of her was grateful she knew how to work hard and was capable of driving a large team.

"Of course," she said.

"*Ach*, the hoppers on the planter aren't big and will need refilling often. You can drive the small wagon with the bags of seed corn," Zeke said.

"All right."

As Abby turned to face forward again, she caught Jakob's glance her way. He seemed deep in thought as he clicked his tongue and gave another slap of the reins.

When they arrived at the Stoltzfuses' farm, Abby sat up straighter and perused the area. Church was held every other week in a member's home. The rustic house was made of large brown logs, so different from the white frame homes Abby was used to back east. The front lawn and flower beds were tidy and well cared for, a tall elm tree offering shade over the front door.

A group of women stood clustered together, chatting. They waved as Jakob drove to the back where a row of buggies were lined up along the inside perimeter of the fence. A teenage boy drew their attention, pointing to where they should park. As Jakob pulled the horse to a halt, another boy began unhitching the animal, then took it away to graze and water until the *familye* was ready to go home.

Jakob hopped out first, then helped his grandfather and mother. Abby didn't wait before climbing down, then reached inside to help Ruby. The girl held her torn skirt together, glancing around nervously to see if anyone was witnessing her embarrassing circumstances.

"There's *Aent* Ruth and *Onkel* Will." Reuben raced toward a young man and obviously pregnant woman.

Reaching for her basket, which contained a pie and two loaves of bread, Naomi smiled at Abby. "Now you'll get to meet my daughter Ruth."

Holding Ruby's hand, Abby followed Naomi toward the house. Men wearing frock coats stood clustered near the barn. Their mixture of black felt and straw hats indicated that the weather was transitioning from winter to spring. Zeke and Jakob headed that way, shaking hands with Will.

Children raced across the yard. Reuben joined the little boys, their boisterous laughter winning a reprimand from one of the mothers.

"How many families are in your congregation?" Abby asked.

"Nine. We're a small district, but we're growing fast," Naomi said.

Hmm. Abby wasn't so sure. In Ohio, her congregation consisted of thirty families. This definitely was a small district, which could be good and bad.

"*Mamm*, it's good to see you." Ruth embraced first her mother and then Ruby.

Abby caught several curious looks thrown her way, especially from the younger, unshaven men, who were obviously unmarried.

"Look at my dress," Ruby whispered as she huddled next to her grandmother and showed a peek of her torn skirt to her aunt.

Ruth gasped and shielded the girl from view. "What happened! You can't go to church like that."

"I don't know what happened. I must have snagged it on something. Abby's gonna fix it for me," Ruby said.

Naomi made the introductions. "Ruth is my youngest, expecting her first child in a few months."

"*Hallo,*" Ruth said, her nose crinkling as she squinted against the bright sunlight.

Abby returned the young woman's gracious smile and glanced down before speaking very quietly so no one would overhear. "You must be so excited to start your *familye*."

Ruth lifted a hand to rest on her rounding stomach and whispered back. "I am. I'm only five months along, but this baby is so active, I'm thinking it must be an unruly boy like Reuben."

They laughed and Abby's heart pinched at the thought of having her own sweet little baby.

"Come on. You promised to fix my dress." Ruby pulled on Abby's hand, and they all went inside the house.

"Guder daag!" A matronly woman with rosy cheeks and a thick waist greeted them from the kitchen.

"Fannie." Naomi rushed over and hugged the woman, then leaned close and whispered in her ear.

Fannie glanced at Ruby. *"Ja*, we'll get her dress mended in no time."

Naomi smiled in relief. Several other women and a few older girls were bustling about the room, stirring pots on the stove, checking the oven and setting out plates and utensils for their noon meal later on. Naomi introduced Abby to everyone, and they gave her a friendly smile.

"Willkomm. We're so glad to have you here," Fannie said.

"I'm glad to be here." Abby nodded pleasantly, then zeroed in on Lizzie Beiler, the young woman she had met at the bakery a couple of days earlier. Lizzie was frosting a chocolate cake, but Fannie whispered something to her and she handed over her spatula.

"*Hallo*, Abby. I understand you need a needle and thread," Lizzie said.

Ruby nodded eagerly, looking a little anxious. She obviously didn't want the meeting to start before her skirt had been repaired.

"*Ja*, if you wouldn't mind," Abby said.

"Not at all. *Koom* with me." Lizzie led them to the back of the house, where she closed a hall door to give them some privacy. It seemed she knew her way around this home with ease.

"Do you live here?" Abby asked, knowing her last name was Beiler, not Stoltzfus.

"*Ne*, but I had planned to live here one day. I'm quite close with Fannie and still come here often." Lizzie's words were slightly muffled as she reached into a cupboard and pulled out a sewing box.

"Are you related to Fannie?" Abby wouldn't be surprised if she was. Many of the Amish in a district were related in some way or another. Aunts, cousins, brothers, nephews. In Ohio, they all lived nearby. But here in Colorado, it wasn't quite the same. Not with its high mountain peaks, deep canyons, wide plateaus and desert valleys that constantly hungered for rain to irrigate crops. Farms were spread far apart, and most of their kin relations had remained back east. They were true pioneers, starting a new life in the Wild West.

"*Ne*, I was engaged to her son, Eli. But he disappeared several years ago, the day before we were to be baptized."

"I'm so sorry to hear that," Abby said.

"He just left without a word to anyone. His parents received a letter from him a week later. He went to Denver, to go to college there."

Abby caught a note of bitterness in Lizzie's voice and couldn't help feeling sympathy for her. "I'm so sorry. That must have hurt you very deeply."

As she assessed Ruby's dress so that she could mend the seam, she remembered what Naomi had said about Eli Stoltzfus breaking Lizzie's heart. No doubt Lizzie had been close with Eli's parents.

"*Ja*, it did. I was baptized without him." Lizzie sat on the bed and threaded a needle before putting a knot in the end. She handed it over to Abby, who also sat and quickly stitched the ripped seam.

"Perhaps you will marry someone else. I understand there are several young men needing brides here in the Riverton area, or perhaps you could find someone in Westcliffe," Abby said, conscious of Ruby standing in front of her listening quietly to every word.

"*Ne*, there's no one here that I'm interested in. And what about you?"

Abby didn't look up from her needlework. "What about me?"

Out of her peripheral vision, Abby saw Lizzie cast a quick glance at Ruby, who was peering out the window.

"Jakob is handsome and single," Lizzie whispered low. "Are you going to marry him?"

Not wanting Ruby to take offense at their conversation, Abby shook her head.

"My father keeps threatening to send me back east to live with my grandparents. He believes I could find someone to marry there, but he hasn't made me go yet," Lizzie said, her forehead crinkled in a doubtful frown.

Abby inwardly shuddered at the thought of returning to Ohio, but for different reasons. She didn't get the chance to ask Lizzie if she wanted to go back east. A knock sounded on the door, and Naomi poked her head in.

"Are you ready? They're about to begin the meeting."

"Just finished." Abby bit the thread with her teeth and smoothed the dress to study her handiwork. "It's as good as new."

Ruby hugged her tight. "*Ach*, *danke*, Abby."

Abby breathed the girl in, enjoying her sweet innocence. "You're welcome."

"*Koom* on, you three," Naomi urged.

Ruby bolted toward her grandmother while Abby quickly restored the sewing box to order. She followed Lizzie outside and into the yard. The married women were lined up by age beside the barn. Naomi took her place among them as they filed inside. Through the wide double doors, Abby saw that the married men were already sitting together on hard backless benches. The unmarried women filed in next, and Lizzie took Abby's hand as they scurried forward. As they paraded down the aisle, Abby was conscious of people watching her. Finally, the unmarried men and boys joined them. One tall young man with bright auburn hair and piercing blue eyes smiled wide at Abby, and she looked away, making a pretense of straightening her apron.

The men sat together on the other side of the room, facing the women. As Abby tidied her skirts, she looked up. Her gaze locked with Jakob's from where he sat across from her. He quickly looked away, focusing on the bishop, who stood at the front of the room. The auburn-haired man continued to stare openly at her, leaning across a row to whisper to Jakob. The two spoke together for a moment and Jakob's gaze lifted to her, then he responded to the auburn-haired man. She had no doubt they were discussing her, and she didn't like it. No, not one bit.

The *vorsinger* called out the first note of the opening song in a loud, elongated voice. The congregation joined in, singing in German from the *Ausbund*, their church hymnal. Without the accompaniment of musical instruments, they drew each note out in a painstakingly slow harmony.

Abby knew the words by heart, but she faltered. The auburn-haired man kept watching her until she became so uncomfortable that she squirmed on her seat. Feeling suddenly miserable, she looked up and caught Jakob's eye again. He looked down, focusing on the floor, and she felt even worse. He must find her so distasteful that he couldn't even stand to look at her.

"The man with the red hair is Martin Hostetler," Lizzie whispered for her ears alone. "He watches all the unmarried girls. He's twenty-three and wants to get married so bad, but he's too pushy. I'm kind of glad you're here so he'll have someone else to bother instead of me."

"Gee, thanks," Abby said, trying not to smile.

Lizzie laughed low. "Just ignore him. That's what I always do."

Abby tried. She really did. But as she watched the ministers file out of the room to discuss who should preach to them, she wondered if she should have pleaded a sick stomach and stayed home today. Between Reuben's open dislike of her, Martin's rude gawking and Jakob's obvious discomfort with her presence, she wondered if perhaps she should have remained in Ohio.

"Please say you'll go to the singing with me tonight. I'll drive you home in my buggy afterward."

Jakob tried to pretend he hadn't heard the invitation, but he couldn't help it. Martin Hostetler stood in front of Abby, no more than a stone's throw away. She held a plate of schnitz apple pie she'd retrieved for *Dawdi* Zeke. Martin had cut her off as she headed across the front lawn.

Zeke sat in a chair on the lawn, deep in conversation with several other elderly men. Martin had been dogging Abby's heels ever since they'd ended their meetings and started lunch. As she helped serve the noon meal, Jakob noticed how easily she fit in with the other women, but she was overly quiet and skittish around the men. Especially Martin, who wouldn't seem to leave her alone. No doubt he was delighted to find an attractive single woman in their midst.

"I'm sorry, but not today." Abby turned toward *Dawdi* Zeke, but Martin tugged on her sleeve, holding her back.

"Why not? Jakob said you're not attached to anyone. Why won't you go with me to the singing?" Martin persisted.

The singing was a venue after Sunday meetings where young single adults could socialize with one another. Afterward, the young man usually took the young woman home in his buggy...the Amish version of dating.

"I... I'm new here and I don't know anyone yet. I think it would be best if I go home with the Fishers this afternoon. Perhaps another time." Her voice sounded low and hesitant, as though she was afraid of angering him.

"*Ach*, how can you get to know any of us if you don't stay for the singing? It'll be fun. You must stay. I insist," Martin said, taking a step closer.

"I... I don't..." Abby didn't finish her sentence. Her face flushed red, a blaze of panic in her eyes. She backed up against the elm tree and hunched her shoulders, looking small and helpless.

Subdued.

"*Ahem*, excuse me." Jakob interrupted them

in a polite voice. "I think Naomi is looking for you, Abby. She needs you in the kitchen."

"*Ach!* I should be helping her, not standing here visiting." She glanced at Martin. "I won't be able to join you tonight, but it was nice to meet you. *Mach's gut.*"

She spoke so fast that Martin looked startled for a moment.

"Uh, maybe another time." He waved at her already-retreating back.

She hurried toward the house. Jakob followed, walking beside her, just in case Martin decided to pursue her. A teenage boy bumped into Abby, and she jerked back.

"Excuse me," she said.

He looked mildly embarrassed before racing off with his friends.

Abby kept going. At the side of the house, she slowed her pace and took a deep inhale.

"Are you all right?" Jakob asked.

"*Ja*, I'm just a little nervous around crowds of strangers."

"I hope it was all right for me to interrupt you and Martin," he said, almost positive that she had wanted to get away from the man.

"*Ja*, I'm glad you did."

"He wasn't bothering you, was he? I know Martin can be a little forceful, but he means well," Jakob said.

She paused at the door leading into the kitchen. "*Ne*, I'm fine. *Danke* for rescuing me," she said.

"I'm just returning the favor. *Danke* for helping my *mudder*. You're right. She's overly tired. You've been a great benefit to her." He spoke low, for her ears alone.

Abby leaned slightly closer and gave him a conspiratorial smile. "You're *willkomm*, although helping Naomi is easy. She's so kind. I wish…"

Again, she didn't finish her thought.

"You wish what?" he pressed.

"Oh, nothing."

He let it go, but a part of him wondered if she was going to say that she wished she'd had a mother like Naomi.

"How old were you when your *mamm* died?" he asked instead.

"I was six. I don't remember her very well. Just bits and pieces, really. I know she loved me, because I remember her comforting me once after my *vadder*…" She shrugged.

After her father did what? Beat her?

"Life must have been difficult for you growing up," he said, trying to imagine what she'd been through.

She met his eyes, still holding the plate of

pie. "I guess it does no good to pretend with you. You already know the truth."

"*Ja*, I know."

"You...you won't tell anyone, will you?" She peered askance at him, as though she'd done something wrong and was embarrassed by it.

"Of course not. It wasn't your fault. Remember that time when I broke the stick over my knee?"

She looked at the ground, not replying.

"I can understand why you're uneasy around men," he said.

She whipped her head up, biting her bottom lip. "Is it that obvious?"

"Only to me, because I know what happened. And I'm sorry for it."

"Don't be. It wasn't your fault either," she said.

And yet, a part of him wished his *familye* hadn't moved away. That he could have stayed in Ohio and been there to intercede for her more often. It seemed he'd always been her protector of sorts. For some reason, it came naturally to him. But if he hadn't moved to Colorado, he never would have met Susan. Never would have known the exquisite love they had shared; never would have had his two beautiful children. Or at least, he didn't think so.

"You must be very angry at your *vadder* and Simon," he said.

She released a long sigh. "I was when I was very young, but not anymore. Simon is what my *vadder* created of him. He didn't know anything else. But the anger has to stop somewhere, so why not with me? Besides, the Lord has sustained me through it all. In my loneliest moments, He has been there beside me."

"You're not angry at *Gott*?" he asked.

"*Ne*, why should I be? I found comfort knowing He was there. And though I don't always understand His plans, He has brought me here to Colorado, where I can have a fresh start."

Jakob caught the conviction in her voice. He couldn't imagine ever reprimanding this woman, even when she was a mischievous child. If anyone tried to hurt Ruby, he'd be furious. And yet, anger wasn't what *Gott* expected from him. Even after losing Susan and his father, Jakob knew he should forgive *Gott* and turn the other cheek. He should have more faith.

"Will you take this to *Dawdi* Zeke for me? I didn't get the chance, and he's expecting it." She held up the pie.

"Of course." He took the plate from her hands, watching as she turned and slipped into the house.

A feeling of compassion swept over him, but something else, as well. Respect and admiration.

"*Hallo*, Jakob."

He turned. Bishop Yoder stood behind him, still wearing his frock coat.

"Bishop." Jakob nodded respectfully.

"Did you enjoy the meetings today?"

"*Ja*, very much." Which was true. Jakob loved being with people of his own faith. But honestly, he could remember very little of the sermons. His thoughts had been centered almost entirely on Abby.

The older man jutted his chin toward the house. "I couldn't help noticing that you were just speaking with Abby."

"*Ja*, she just went inside to help my *mudder* in the kitchen."

"How are things working out with her living in your home?"

"*Gut*. She is a great help on the farm."

"Have you reconsidered a possible marriage with her?"

Jakob blinked. He hadn't expected the bishop to be so blunt. "I'm afraid nothing has changed. I still love Susan. I can't consider marrying another woman anytime soon."

Bishop Yoder lowered his head for several moments, as though thinking how to respond.

Then, he spoke in a soft, kind voice. "Before He was crucified, the Savior gave His apostles a new commandment that they should love one another. That commandment extends to us, as well. The Lord's capacity to love was absolute, unconditional and unrestrained. As we treat one another with service, compassion and respect, our love increases. It isn't limited, and it never runs out."

Jakob was speechless. What was the bishop saying? That if he treated Abby with service, compassion and respect, he would love her? That might be true, but he couldn't love her as a man should love his wife. Not a romantic love. When Susan had died, Jakob had felt bewildered, confused and frightened. He was stuck in limbo and couldn't seem to move past her memory.

"Would you still have married Susan, even knowing that you would lose her one day?" the bishop asked.

Jakob nodded without hesitation. "Absolutely."

"Then would you say that loving and being with her even for a short time was worth the pain of losing her?"

Again, Jakob wondered what the bishop was getting at. He didn't like to play mind games.

"*Ja*, I would do it all over again, even knowing ~~that I would lose her one day.~~"

"She would want you to be happy, Jakob. Don't be afraid to love again," the bishop said.

Afraid? Jakob wasn't afraid. Not really. Okay, maybe a little bit. He was afraid of loving and losing again. He couldn't go through that trauma a second time, and he didn't want to put his children through it either.

The bishop glanced to where Martin stood conversing with several young men his age. "I also noticed Abby speaking with Martin Hostetler. I know he is eager to find a wife, and he seems very interested in her."

"*Ja*, he asked her to stay for the singing time with him, but she declined."

Jakob felt a bit defensive. He didn't want Abby to spend time with the other man, but that wasn't fair. She was young and pretty and should have some fun. She deserved all the joy this world could offer. And Martin was a nice enough man. He deserved to be happy, too.

Bishop Yoder shrugged. "She is still new here, but that will soon change. One day, some smart young man will realize that she's worth it, too."

Jakob caught the hint, but it didn't make a difference. Not for him. Abby would make some other man a fine wife. A kind, patient man she could love and grow old with.

He thought it was ironic that she didn't blame *Gott* for the sadness in her life. Instead, she relied on the Lord. Her faith sustained her. In contrast, Jakob's faith had faltered. Losing his wife and father had devastated him. He'd felt abandoned and lost. Angry even. Perhaps he could learn some valuable lessons from Abby's humble heart. But marriage to her? Definitely not.

Chapter Seven

The next morning, Abby stepped out onto the back porch and picked up the wire basket they used to collect eggs. Sunlight streamed across the yard, chasing the chill out of the spring air.

Inside the house, she could hear Naomi humming as she sorted laundry. Jakob had driven Reuben to school in the buggy. As usual, the boy had scowled deeply when he discovered that Abby had prepared his lunch. Once again, she'd written an uplifting note and hidden it in his sandwich wrapper where he was sure to find it. Hopefully it would help soften his heart toward her.

Crossing the yard, she headed for the chicken coop, swinging the wire basket beside her. She would get the barn chores done before she needed to help Jakob plant the field corn.

As she passed the barn, she heard a faint

sound, almost like the cry of a child. She looked up. The door to the hayloft stood wide open, and she thought Jakob must be airing it out after the long winter. Soon, the fields would be burgeoning with newly planted corn and hay. Tomorrow or the next day, she would plant carrots, beets and peas. Each vegetable did well in cooler climates. She'd have to wait a bit longer to plant tomatoes and squash.

The sound came again and she paused, listening for a moment. Hmm, she must be imagining things.

Continuing on her way to the coop, she let herself inside. The musty smell of chickens and dust made her nose twitch. She gazed through the dim interior, noticing that all but one hen had vacated their nests. The remaining chicken gave a disgruntled cluck and tilted its head, staring at Abby with its dark, beady eyes.

"You're a slowpoke today. But don't worry. I'll give you some extra time before I take your eggs," Abby promised with a soft laugh.

The hen clucked again, as though in agreement. Abby searched the other nests first, placing the white and brown eggs carefully in her basket. She worked quickly, removing any wood shavings from the nests that were particularly dirty and replacing them with fresh

straw. When she was finished, she looked at the
~~mother hen and rested one hand on her waist.~~

"Aren't you finished yet? Or are you going
to stay there all day?" Abby asked.

The red hen just stared back at her.

Moving gently but quickly, Abby lifted the
hen and removed the eggs from her nest. The
hen barely noticed, and Abby smiled with satisfaction.

"I'm all done. I'll see you later this evening,
and I hope you're off the nest by that time."

With her basket filled, Abby stepped outside
into the sunlight and closed the door. As she se-
cured the latch on the hen house, she heard the
strange sound again. A faint *mewl* that died off
quickly. Definitely not from a child. More like
a little animal. But where was it coming from?

There! She heard it again, more softly this
time.

Entering the barn, Abby set her egg basket aside on a high shelf. Dust motes floated
through cracks in the walls, the faint sunlight
filtering through the dim interior. A subtle rustling came from the hayloft. Abby gazed up at
the long, arching timbers curving across the
ceiling like the skeleton of a giant whale's rib
cage. Even her father's barn in Ohio wasn't this

large and spacious. She couldn't help being impressed by Jakob's construction skills.

A tall ladder reached up to the loft. Lifting her skirts away from her ankles, she stepped on the bottom rung and started to climb. Her skirt got twisted around her shoe and she lost her footing. Gripping the side of the ladder, she caught herself just in time and untangled her skirt.

"Ouch!"

Several splinters from the rough timber had dug their way into her fingers. As she reached to pull them out, she lost her balance and fell backward.

Strong arms suddenly wrapped around her. For just a fraction of time, she felt a solid chest at her back and a warm cheek pressed against her own.

"Oh!" She jerked away so fast that Jakob stumbled and grabbed for the ladder to catch himself.

He looked at her, his eyes wide with surprise. "Are you all right?"

She breathed heavily, trying to catch her breath. "*Ja*, I'm fine."

But no, she wasn't. Not really. She felt mortified by the physical contact they had shared.

"Are you certain? You seem flustered. I was only trying to save you from a bad fall," he said.

"I'm sorry. I guess I've developed quick reflexes. I learned at a young age to be on my guard."

He accepted her admittance without comment, but she could tell from his expression that he understood. Living with her father and Simon had taught her to duck fast at a moment's notice.

"Let me see the damage," he said.

She didn't fight him as he took her hand in his, perusing her injury with infinite tenderness. The skin on his palms was roughened by hard work, but his fingers were warm and gentle. Using his blunt fingernails, he plucked out two of the splinters.

"I'm afraid I can't get the last one out, but *Mamm* has a pair of tweezers in the house that you can use," he said.

He released her hand and she folded her hands together, looking down. *"Danke."*

As she glanced at him, her entire body heated up as hot as Naomi's woodstove. She lifted a hand to her face where she still felt the warmth of his cheek. He stood in front of her in his worn work clothes, looking strong and handsome, yet completely harmless. She followed the movement of his hand as he reached up and rubbed his beard.

"What were you doing up on the ladder anyway?" He glanced toward the loft.

"I… I heard mewling sounds and wanted to see if Ruby's barn cat was up there." She took another step back, trying to calm her racing heart. She told herself she didn't need to fear this man, but the jittery instinct to run and hide was difficult to resist.

Jakob shook his head, his eyes creased with stoic sorrow. "I'm afraid Amber is gone."

"Gone where?" she asked, remembering that Amber was the name of Ruby's cat.

"I found her on the side of the highway this morning on my way home from taking Reuben to school. She'd been hit by a car. I just buried her so the children wouldn't see."

"Oh, *ne*." Abby covered her mouth with one hand, her heart filled with sadness. She'd seen how vehicles whizzed by on the road, moving so fast that the drivers could barely notice anything in their path. It reaffirmed Abby's preference for buggies and horses, which moved at a calm, sane speed.

"Will you tell Ruby that her cat is gone?" she asked, her voice wobbling slightly.

"*Ja*, both *kinder* will have to be told. Ruby lives on a farm and understands such things, but I know she'll be upset."

Abby agreed, but didn't get the chance to say

so. The mewling sound came again, such a piti-
ful, weak cry that they could have easily missed
it if they'd been talking at that precise moment.

Jakob tilted his head, his gaze lifting to the
stacks of hay above. "I just heard it, too. I wonder…"

Without finishing his thought, he set his foot
on the bottom rung of the ladder and hurried
up. Abby waited below. Was it possible that
Amber had her kittens up there? When Abby
thought about the babies without their mother
to care for them, a sense of urgency swept over
her. She took a deep inhale and held it for several seconds. When Jakob reappeared, she let
it go.

"What did you find?" she asked.

He didn't reply as he climbed down. When
he reached the bottom, she noticed he gripped
the ladder with one hand, his other hand held
close against his chest.

Safely on his feet, he turned and revealed two
baby kittens so small that he could easily hold
them with one hand. A miniature head with
teensy ears poked up, showing white fur with
one yellow and one gray spot on top. The second kitten had yellow and gray stripes. Both
babies peered at her with large blue eyes. Completely defenseless and adorable.

Abby reached to pet them, unable to stop

herself. "*Ach*, how precious. How old do you think they are?"

"Their eyes are open, but they're wobbly when they walk. I'd say they're about two weeks old, which fits with when Amber stopped coming to the house at night. No doubt she's been busy tending to her babies."

Abby's maternal instincts kicked in. "They're weak. Who knows how long it's been since they were fed last."

"*Ja*, if they don't eat soon, they won't make it. Babies this young can't last long without food."

"You're right. Please, let me help them, Jakob. They'll make good barn cats and catch lots of mice. I can take care of them and finish all my chores, too. They won't be any trouble at all, and I'll keep them out of your way. I promise." She peered at his face, awaiting his reaction.

His forehead crinkled in confusion. "You don't need to defend them to me, Abby. Of course we'll take care of these babies. Do you expect me to just let them die?"

She realized her mistake. This was not her brother she was talking with. "*Ne*, of course not. I... I wasn't sure what you thought."

"I would never do anything to hurt these kittens, unless I couldn't prevent it."

Of course not. He wasn't cruel, like Simon.

His reassurance bolstered her courage and she took the white kitten from him, cuddling it close to her chest. "Does Ruby have any doll bottles?"

"I don't think so." He turned, searching the barn until he found a wooden crate.

"What about a medicine dropper? I can feed the babies with that," she said.

"*Ja*, I believe we have a small dropper. And some old towels we can put in the bottom of this crate."

"Would Naomi mind if we take the kittens inside the kitchen where it's warm? The best place would be right next to the woodstove," she said, hoping she wasn't pushing his patience too far.

"*Ne, Mamm* wouldn't mind at all. In fact, I think she'll be happy that we found Amber's babies."

Carrying the crate and striped kitten, he headed toward the house with Abby following behind. She snatched up the basket of eggs along her way. As they crossed the yard, she was touched by Jakob's kindness. Simon would have yelled and screamed. He wouldn't have wanted to be bothered by a couple of orphaned kittens. He would have even forbidden her to care for them. She knew, because it had happened once before, and she'd been heartsick over the loss.

Even though Jakob had been kind to her, Abby kept forgetting that he was of a different caliber from her brother. And for just a moment, she wished things could be different between them.

"*Ach*, the poor dears," Naomi cried when she found out what had happened.

"It's a blessing that you found them in time," *Dawdi* Zeke said, peering over his great-granddaughter's shoulder.

Ruby snuggled the white kitten close to her pinafore, her eyes filled with tears. "You won't let them die, will you, *Daed*?"

"We'll take *gut* care of the babies, but their lives are in *Gott's* hands." Jakob handed a dropper he'd found in the medicine cabinet to Abby after removing the final splinter in her finger using his *mamm's* tweezers.

She'd already placed a pan of goat's milk and a little Karo syrup on the stove to warm. After washing the dropper and sterilizing it, she handed it to Naomi. The older woman cuddled the white kitten in the crook of her left arm. The poor animal was too weak to even struggle. After sucking milk into the dropper, Naomi introduced it to the kitten's mouth. At first, the baby resisted and milk dripped onto its fur. Naomi persisted and the kitten soon caught on. It suckled the milk greedily. They all stood around, watching with amazement. Finally, the baby's stomach was round and taut. The kitten yawned, its pink tongue curling back in its little mouth.

While Abby cleaned and sterilized the dropper a second time, Zeke took the full kitten and placed it gently in the nest of warm towels in the crate beside the stove. The baby curled up and almost instantly fell asleep.

"See there. That's a good sign," he said.

"We'll need something more than a medicine dropper to feed these hungry babies. I think we need to go into town to the feed and grain store and see if we can buy a couple of nursing kits. I've seen them there before," Jakob said.

Abby handed the cleaned dropper to Naomi. "I can pay for whatever we need."

"You'll do no such thing," Naomi said as she took the striped kitten from Ruby. The baby mewed pathetically. "We will buy the nursing kits, although I think it'll take all of us to keep these newborns fed. I suspect they'll need to eat every hour or so for the time being. They're very young."

"How do you know what to feed them?"

Ruby asked Abby, watching with wide eyes as her grandmother fed the baby.

"My sister-in-law taught me. We found an orphaned kitten on our farm once..." Abby's voice drifted off, a sad look in her eyes.

Jakob wondered if the kitten had died. Something about her voice and the way she'd begged him to let her care for the babies led him to guess that Simon hadn't been too supportive. It would be foolish to let an animal die if you could do something to save it. On a farm, all the animals served a purpose and helped with the prosperity of the place, even barn cats. But Simon wasn't the type of man to care, which might account for why his farm had never done very well.

"Goat's milk won't be enough. It will only tide the babies over until we can go into town and buy some kitten formula at the pet store," Abby said.

Ruby looked at her father, the ribbons on her *kapp* bobbing with her head. "Can you go now, *Daed*? We have to get the babies some *gut* food or they'll die."

Jakob smiled, wanting to reassure his daughter. "Don't worry. I'll go this afternoon, when I pick Reuben up from school. The goat's milk will work fine until then. In the meantime, I need to go outside and plant corn. But I'll return in time to go into town."

Ruby threw her arms around his waist and hugged him tightly. *"Danke, Daedi."*

He kissed her cheek, delighted by her tender heart. She was so much like her mother. Over the top of her head, he saw the gratitude shining in Abby's eyes. For some reason, he wanted to prove to her that he wasn't like her brother. That he was a better man than that.

Without its sibling and mother's warm body to keep it company, the white kitten began to cry. Abby picked it up and held the baby close.

She giggled. "Its fur tickles my nose."

"Let me see," Ruby said.

Abby lowered the kitten so that the girl could rub her face against its fur. Ruby squealed with delight, and they all laughed. Jakob stared at Abby, mesmerized by the way her smile made her blue eyes glitter.

"It has a yellow spot on its head," Ruby said.

"Ja, it's the same color as your *mudder's* daffodils. Maybe that would be a good name for the kitten," Abby suggested.

Ruby nodded. *"Ja*, I'll call this baby Daffy. *Mamm* called her daffodils the daffies."

"Daffy." Abby said the name, as if trying it out on her tongue. "It's perfect. I like it."

"So do I," *Dawdi* Zeke said.

"Reuben can name the other kitten," Ruby suggested.

"That sounds fair," Naomi said.

Jakob watched them all. Abby's eyes glowed with happiness. Sunlight filtered through the window, highlighting wisps of golden hair that had come free of her white *kapp*. He was surprised that she would suggest they name one of the kittens after Susan's flowers, but he was fast learning that Abby was both generous and compassionate. She didn't seem to feel threatened by Susan's memory at all. And her laughter did something to him inside. Something he didn't understand. When they'd been out in the barn and she'd confided how she'd acquired fast reflexes, her admission reaffirmed his desire to shield her from harm. There was no way he could ever refuse her request to care for the kittens. In fact, he wondered if he could refuse her anything.

"I'd better get out to the fields," he said.

"I'll come help," Abby said.

"No need yet. Bring the smaller seed wagon out in a couple of hours. By then, I'll be ready to refill the hoppers."

She nodded, reaching for the eggs she'd gathered. He knew she would clean and put them in the well house, to keep them cool. Naomi would use many of them for her baking, but they would sell the remainder to the country store in town. Another cash crop that brought funds into the household.

"I'll help out here. I may be shaky, but I can still hold a baby kitten," *Dawdi* Zeke said. A deep smile creased the elderly man's face as he watched the striped kitten sleep.

Abby filled a basin with warm water, and Jakob forced himself to turn away. He longed to stay right here and enjoy this quiet interlude with his *familye*, but there was work to be done. He couldn't spend the day ogling baby kittens with Abby.

Chapter Eight

In exactly two hours, Abby hitched up Tommy, the *familye's* chestnut gelding. Naomi was hanging laundry on the line and had a batch of bread in the oven. Abby waved as she pulled away from the barn.

Jakob had already stacked bags of seed corn in the back of the small wagon. His thoughtfulness pleased her. Simon would have made her lift the heavy bags.

As she headed toward the fields, she could see Jakob driving four Belgian draft horses hitched to a four-row planter. Standing on the platform, he wore his straw hat as he glanced over his shoulder often to ensure the seed corn was dispensing correctly. With his strong hands holding the lead lines, he moved the big horses at an even pace, the furrows long and straight. As her wagon bumped over the uneven ground, she couldn't help admiring Jakob's muscular back and arms.

She pulled off to the side of the field, leaving him enough room to turn his team around. When he reached the end of the column, she noticed a perplexed frown on his face.

He pulled the Belgians to a halt, then hopped down and went to peruse the machinery. He bent over and fidgeted with one of the seed units for a moment, then released a low huff of air. He stood straight and shook his head, holding something in his hands.

Abby jumped down and joined him.

"Is something wrong?" she asked.

He whipped his hat off and wiped his brow with his forearm, then held up a chain that was blackened with oil. "*Ja*, one of the drive chains broke. This is a new field and very rocky ground. I can't finish planting until the chain is replaced."

She could see the frustration etched across his face. No doubt he was eager to finish the planting, but that might not happen today.

"What can I do to help?" she asked.

He glanced upward at the position of the sun. "It appears we'll be going into town now. Things might move faster if you rode with me. While I get the replacement chain, you can get the nursing kits and formula for the kittens.

Then we can pick up Reuben from school on the way back. If I can get the chain replaced today, I can finish planting tomorrow."

She paused, surprised that he would invite her to ride into town with him. No doubt Ruby would prefer to remain at home to tend the kittens. But Abby quickly reminded herself that this was just work. Jakob needed her help, nothing more.

"Of course I'll go. I'm happy to help," she said.

He walked around the corn planter so he could unhitch the team. She didn't need to ask why. It would not be prudent to leave the horses standing out in the hot sun while they made the long trip into town.

As he undid the chains on the tug lines, one of the horses thrust his left hind foot back, striking Jakob on the back of his lower leg. It happened so fast that neither of them saw it coming.

"Oof!" The man dropped to the ground like stone, his straw hat falling off his head.

"Jakob!" Abby raced to his side, frightened that he'd be trampled by the horses.

She pulled on his arms until he was a safe distance away from the giant Belgians. He lay flat on his back, his eyes closed, a grimace of agony on his face as he pulled his injured leg up toward his chest.

"Are you all right?" She touched his pale cheek with one hand, praying that he wasn't injured seriously.

"*Ja*, I... I think I'm all right." His voice sounded tight and breathless as he struggled to sit up.

She helped him, her gaze lowering to his leg. "*Ne*, you're hurt."

Gritting his teeth, he rolled up his pant leg and rotated his calf to show an ugly red mark in the shape of a horseshoe across his flesh. It was swelling right before their eyes.

"You're going to have a nasty bruise," she said.

"*Ja*, Billy clipped me good this time. He has a nasty habit of doing that. I was in too big a hurry and let my guard down," Jakob remarked, breathing heavily.

"Can you stand?" Abby asked, reaching her arm around to support his back. She caught his scent, a subtle mixture of horses and Naomi's homemade soap made with coconut oil.

He nodded and gritted his teeth as he stood with effort. When he tried to put weight on his injured leg, a guttural groan came from his throat. He faltered, holding on tight to Abby.

"It might be broken," she said.

"Heaven help us if it is. I've got to get these fields planted. I can't be laid up right now." His voice sounded roughened by fear and pain.

Abby didn't need to ask why. They had a few days' leeway, but if they didn't get the crops planted, they would have nothing to harvest and no livelihood for the following year. Other men might be able to help, but their Amish community was not large and everyone was busy planting their own fields.

"Don't you worry," she said. "No matter what, we'll take care of it somehow. If nothing else, I've planted fields on my own before. I can do it again."

For some reason, she wanted to reassure him. She knew how it felt to be desperate and alone, and she didn't want Jakob to feel that way when he was in pain.

He jerked his head up in surprise, a jagged thatch of hair falling into his eyes. "Your brother made you do the planting alone? Without his help?"

She couldn't resist showing a wry smile. "*Ja.* Knowing Simon, are you really so surprised?"

He pursed his lips with disapproval but didn't respond. With her aid, he hopped over to the small wagon, and she helped him pull himself into the seat. After retrieving his hat, she scampered up beside him and drove them to the

house. Within minutes, she'd raced inside to tell
~~Naomi what had happened.~~ They asked Ruby to
stay in the kitchen, to watch the kittens. There
was no sense in making Jakob hobble into the
house if they had to take him to the clinic in
town. He remained in the wagon while Naomi
inspected the burgeoning bruise. It had spread
and was already turning an angry black color.

"That mean ole horse. You ought to get rid
of him, Jakob. He nearly broke your *vadder's*
arm once," Naomi said as she gently touched
the tight skin with her fingertips.

"Billy isn't mean—he's just skittish. He's
still the strongest horse on the farm and we're
not getting rid of him," Jakob replied between
gritted teeth.

"*Ach*, I still wish you'd trade him for another,
gentler horse," she said.

Jakob didn't reply. His jaw was locked, his
hands clenched. Abby could tell he was in ter-
rible pain, yet he spoke with complete calm,
his voice soft and even.

"Do you think his leg is broken?" Abby
asked.

Naomi shook her head. "There's no way of
knowing for sure. It could have just bruised the
bone, or torn the muscle. With the fields needing to be planted, we can't take the chance. You
better drive him into town for an X-ray."

Without a word, Abby unloaded the heavy bags of seed corn from the back of the wagon. The gelding certainly couldn't travel quickly into town while pulling such a heavy load. She had just finished the chore when Zeke appeared from the *dawdy haus*.

"What's going on?" he asked, shambling over to them.

They quickly explained.

"Why didn't you call me to help unload the seed corn from the wagon?" Zeke asked Abby.

"There was no need. I'm strong enough," Abby said. It hadn't been easy, but she knew the work would hurt him much more than it would hurt her. She didn't want to do anything to endanger the elderly man's health.

"I'll bring the Belgians in from the field," Zeke said.

"*Ne*, I'll fetch them," Naomi said. "Abby will take Jakob to the doctor and pick Reuben up on their way home. You stay here and help Ruby with the kittens. If it starts to rain, gather in the laundry."

Since there wasn't a cloud in the sky, Abby doubted the laundry hanging on the line was in any danger of getting rained on. Naomi seemed to know that the simple chore gave Zeke something to occupy himself.

Naomi took off toward the fields before Zeke could argue. As he hobbled toward the house, Abby could hear him grumbling something about getting old, losing respect and being consigned to women's work.

Women frequently drove large teams of horses while their men baled hay. But Naomi wasn't young anymore either, and Abby hated to make her bring the draft horses in from the field. But Naomi had given them no choice. And Abby couldn't help wondering why everyone seemed to want her to go with Jakob instead of letting Naomi drive him into town.

Taking the leads into her hands, Abby slapped them against Tommy's back. Jakob braced his wounded leg against the seat, but his stoic expression told her that he was hurting. To take his mind off the pain, she distracted him with chatter.

"*Danke* for letting us care for the kittens. They'll grow fast and we'll be able to wean them within a few weeks," she said.

"I knew it was important to you. We couldn't just leave them in the hayloft. They would have died," he said.

"*Ja*, there have been times when I've felt alone and helpless, just like those babies. It was you who came to my rescue once," she confessed.

He reached over and squeezed her hand, so suddenly and unexpectedly that she almost gasped.

"Don't worry. We'll do all we can for them. This has been a challenging day, but it'll get better," he said.

She stared at him, surprised at his optimism. He had been injured and was in pain, yet he was comforting her. No accusations. No anger. Just a gentle reassurance.

Looking away, she puzzled over his comments. She was uncertain of his motives. He didn't want to marry her, yet he was always so supportive. A fog of emotions swirled around inside her mind. She trusted and respected this man. He was someone she considered a good friend. But if she wasn't careful, her feelings could easily grow. And loving Jakob would only cause her more grief.

Although the next few hours rushed by for Jakob, it wasn't without considerable discomfort. Abby drove him straight to the only clinic in town. When the horse had kicked him, he'd been blinded by pain so intense that he could hardly breathe. Now, a throbbing ache had settled into his calf, as though his leg were about to explode. He'd feel better if he knew for sure it wasn't broken.

While he received X-rays and an ice pack for his calf, Abby hurried over to the feed and grain store. He'd given her the money and explicit instructions as to the replacement chain she should buy. And when she returned, he was pleased to discover that she'd obtained exactly what he needed to make the repair. She'd also purchased two nursing kits and kitten formula. Thankfully, his leg wasn't broken, but the muscle and surrounding tissue were badly bruised. The doctor advised him to stay off his feet for at least a week, but that wasn't going to happen. The pain would pass, but they had to get their fields planted as soon as possible. Such was the life of a farmer.

On their way home, they stopped and picked Reuben up from school. He stared in silence as Jakob explained all that had transpired throughout the day. As they drove home, Jakob saw the boy casting quick glances at Abby, as though he were seeing her for the first time.

When they arrived home, Abby pulled up out front of the house. With Naomi and *Dawdi* Zeke's support, Jakob limped up the cobblestone sidewalk he'd laid with his own hands years earlier. Glancing over his shoulder, he watched Abby drive the wagon to the barn. Reuben stayed with her, not needing to be asked to help unhitch the horse. The boy's shoulders were tense and he wore a heavy frown, but he didn't say a word. Jakob was relieved to see that his son understood his duties in spite of his personal feelings for Abby. A short time later, Abby and the boy rejoined the rest of the *familye* inside the kitchen.

"Reuben helped me feed and water the horses. I'll do the milking as soon as we've given the babies some kitten formula," Abby said, setting a brown paper sack on the countertop.

"I'll help with the milking," *Dawdi* Zeke said.

"Danke." Sitting in a chair at the table, Jakob had propped his injured leg on another chair to elevate it. Naomi had prepared a fresh cold compress for him. He felt slightly unmanned to turn his evening chores over to Abby, his son and his elderly grandfather, but he was beyond grateful for their willing attitudes.

"I don't know what we would have done without you today," Naomi said to Abby.

"It's the least I can do. You've been so kind to me."

"I'll help with the milking, too." Reuben spoke in a quiet voice.

Jakob noticed the tenderness in his son's eyes as he held each of the kittens.

"I named the white baby Daffy because she

has a yellow spot on her head that matches *Mamm's* daffodils. Abby suggested it," Ruby said. "*Dawdi* thinks she's a girl. You get to name the other kitten. *Dawdi* thinks he's a boy."

Reuben picked up the striped baby, his eyes filled with tender awe. "He's so small. Look at his tiny whiskers. And his claws are so small and sharp. He looks like a little tiger."

"Tiger," *Dawdi* Zeke repeated. "That's a perfect name for a barn cat. No doubt he'll be a good mouser."

Reuben grinned from ear to ear, obviously pleased by the name he'd chosen.

Jakob felt a bit woozy from the pain pill the doctor had given him. Naomi kept urging him to go to the *dawdy haus* and lie down, but he delayed a little longer. Today could have ended in tragedy, and he had a lot to be grateful for. It felt so good to be in the safety of his own home, surrounded by his *familye*. All was well. And yet, something had drastically changed between him and Abby. He wasn't certain what it was and he didn't understand it at all, but he sensed that their relationship had deepened somehow. Surely he was imagining things.

"May I feed Tiger?" Reuben asked Abby in a cautious tone.

She turned from the stove, where she had just heated and filled one of the small bottles from the nursing kit with kitten formula. For just a moment, her eyes widened in surprise, and Jakob realized this was the first time Reuben had addressed her politely.

"Of course you may." She dribbled several drops of milk on her wrist, then nodded at Reuben. "The milk is ready."

"Why did you do that?" the boy asked, indicating her wrist.

"To make sure the milk isn't too hot for the baby's mouth," she said.

Jakob watched as she showed his son how to hold Tiger in the crook of his arm. When she touched him, Reuben tensed but didn't push her away. He jerked when the baby latched on to the bottle a bit ferociously, and they all laughed.

"I can see these kittens have quickly regained their strength. Unless something unforeseen happens, I think they're going to be all right," Naomi said.

"*Ja*, thanks to Abby," Jakob said, unable to deny a warm glow of happiness inside his heart.

"It's a good thing she heard the babies crying and went looking for them in the barn, or we wouldn't have found them in time," *Dawdi* Zeke said.

Reuben glanced at the woman he hadn't yet been able to accept. Abby smiled at him, her expression one of tolerance and compassion, but his face held a skeptical frown. When he gazed at the tiny kitten he held in his arms, his eyes glimmered with love. No doubt he was enamored by the babies.

Once Tiger had eaten his fill, Abby fluffed the towel in the bottom of the wooden crate. Reuben laid Tiger beside Daffy. The two kittens curled together, sharing body heat. And without any warning, Reuben threw his arms around Naomi's waist and hugged her, his face pressed against her side.

"*Danke* for saving the kittens." Reuben's words were muffled against his grandmother's apron, but they all heard him nevertheless.

"You're *willkomm*, but I've done very little. You should be thanking Abby," Naomi said.

The boy looked up at Abby, his eyes filled with doubt. He didn't say a word, just frowned with skepticism.

"You're most *willkomm*, sweetheart," Abby responded anyway.

The boy moved away, brushing at his eyes. If Jakob weren't feeling so fuzzy, he would have thought his son was crying. He was disappointed in the boy. Even a pair of orphaned kittens couldn't convince Reuben to finally become friendly with Abby. Regardless, the kittens had been therapeutic to the grief-stricken *familye*. They had laughed and enjoyed feeding the babies so much. Abby had made a difference in their lives, and Jakob was grateful for her soothing influence in his home. But she still wasn't his beloved wife. Jakob knew it, and so did Reuben. Abby wasn't Susan, and she never would be.

Chapter Nine

"Are you sure you're up to this?" Abby watched dubiously as Jakob limped over to the corn planter.

It sat exactly where they'd left it the day before. As promised, Naomi had brought the draft horses in right after Abby had driven Jakob to the clinic in town. Now, morning sunlight gleamed across the bare ground, highlighting the dark, fertile soil. The day wasn't too hot or cold, but just right for planting.

"It must be done," Jakob said.

Although he was still young, Reuben had joined them in the field. The boy hefted the red toolbox out of the wagon and carried it over to set beside his father on the frame of the planter. Naomi had wanted to help, but Jakob adamantly refused. She wasn't a young woman anymore and the task would be too much for her. Besides, her help wasn't necessary. Not with Abby there.

Jakob reached to open the box but nearly toppled over in the process. He didn't cry out as the movement jarred his leg, but Abby saw the pain written across his face. He wasn't up to this chore either, but he was resolute. No amount of pleading had convinced him to stay in the house. And Abby had to admire his tenacity. He was a man determined to take care of his *familye*.

"Tell me what you need and I'll hand it to you," she said, wishing she knew how to make the repair.

"I'll help, too, *Daed*," Reuben said.

As promised, they all worked together. Jakob stood leaning against the planter, resting his weight on his good leg. Abby placed a socket wrench in his hand, and he loosened a couple of bolts on the sprockets. It took some effort as the bolts were very tight, and Abby was grateful for his strength.

Within minutes, they had the new chain threaded and Jakob tightened down the bolts. When he finished, he turned, stumbled and fell heavily against her.

"Daed!" Reuben cried.

Abby didn't think before wrapping her arms around him, an automatic response. The man grunted, reaching for the planter to steady himself. If Abby hadn't caught him, she knew he would have gone down.

While Abby supported Jakob's right side, Reuben supported his left.

"I think you're finished being on your feet today," Abby said.

"But the planting… I have to get it done," Jakob argued, sounding out of breath.

"We'll get it done, but you will do no more than sit in the wagon and supervise. Reuben and I will do the planting. You're in no position to argue, so don't fight us. Right, Reuben?" She looked pointedly at the boy, seeking his support.

The boy gave a decisive nod of his head. "Right. It's no good to fight us, *Daed*. We only have your well-being in mind."

The boy sounded so grown up. Abby looked away, hiding a satisfied smile. Thinking it would draw them closer, she'd purposefully tried to get Reuben on her side. Her ploy had worked, and the boy grinned at her as they helped Jakob into the wagon. She'd brought a heavy quilt along to elevate and support his leg.

Now that he was off his feet, the man breathed with relief and took the leads into his hands. He drove Abby back to the barn, where she hitched up the Belgians with Reuben's help.

The boy was small, but he knew what to do and was a hard worker. They soon had the draft horses back in the field and hooked up to the corn planter.

"You'll need this." Jakob held out a level to her.

Abby reached up and took the instrument, knowing what it was for. She placed it on the main tool bar of the planter, noticing the bubble was off-kilter. Again, Reuben helped as she made a few adjustments. They pushed, grunted and adjusted the air pressure until the bubble inside the level was even.

"The disc openers were working perfectly yesterday, but you better check them again," Jakob called.

Abby nodded and did as asked. The disc openers were set at an angle so that they would open a furrow for the corn seeds to drop into. The angle was about two inches, and she figured that was perfect.

She glanced at Jakob. "They're good."

"Check the gauge wheels, too," he said.

She did, just barely able to turn them. "The down force is good. I think we're ready to begin."

"Just one more thing. The closing wheels," Reuben said.

Running to the back of the planter, he inspected the wheels. His bare feet sank into the soft soil as he ensured that each set of wheels was angled properly so that they would close the furrows of dirt over the seeds.

Since he was still quite young, Abby joined him. Seeing that all was in order, she asked his opinion, hoping to build his self-confidence. "What do you think? Are they good?"

Reuben nodded, looking very serious and mature for his age. "All is well. We are ready."

"Very *gut*, Reuben. You're so clever to remember to check the closing wheels," Abby praised him.

Reuben beamed as he joined her on the driving platform. With Jakob sitting safely in the shade at the side of the field, Abby took hold of the lead lines. She immediately felt the horses' tremendous strength pulling on the lines. Looking forward, she gazed at four chestnut rumps and flaxen tails, which were attached to a total of eight thousand pounds of horsepower. She'd driven draft animals before, but each horse had a different personality. She didn't know these Belgians at all, except that Billy was skittish enough to badly injure a fully grown man. And here she was, a mere woman trying to command all of this strength with nothing more than the tone of her voice and a strong tug on the lines.

"*Ach*, there's no time like the present," she murmured to herself.

Gathering her courage, she slapped the leads against the horses' backs.

"*Schritt!*" she called, wishing her voice wouldn't tremble so much.

The horses stepped forward, and a lance of joy speared her heart. Reuben gripped the support bar that extended across the platform. He gazed ahead, seeming eager for this adventure they had undertaken. But Abby wasn't. She knew how much they were depending on this harvest. She was desperate not to disappoint Jakob, nor let the *familye* down.

"Haw!" she called.

Lifting her head higher, she tugged on the leads. She almost laughed aloud when the Belgians turned left, just as she'd directed them. She did her best to line up the planter with Jakob's last finished row. Then she lowered the long marker bar. The armature extended out from the planter and traced the next row. She kept glancing at it, to ensure she drove the team straight and created long, even furrows.

Within an hour, she learned that Sally was inclined to jackrabbit starts, but Scottie was a calming influence next to her. Boaz stood on the far right side. He was fast, but he wasn't coming around into the turns as well as Abby would have liked. She slowed the team down a bit to give him time to catch up to the horses on the inside. And Billy might be skittish, but he was the strength of the team. He stabilized the planter, his strong muscles bunching as he pulled nice and even.

The work took all of her concentration, but she was still highly conscious of Jakob watching them from the wagon. She'd expected him to nod off and nap, but he sat straight and tall, his injured leg resting on the bunched-up blanket, his glimmering eyes on the planter. When she turned the team to head the other way, she could almost feel his gaze boring a hole in her back. A memory of Simon watching her with a critical eye rushed over her, along with the fear of his disapproval and a possible beating. She didn't believe Jakob would hurt her, but she felt nervous anyway. She wanted to do a good job for him. She told herself it was because she didn't want him to make her leave, but deep inside she knew it was something more. In spite of his rejection of marriage, she still wanted to ease his mind and make him happy.

By late afternoon, Jakob was worried. At midday, Abby had insisted she was doing fine. Reuben had eaten his bologna-and-cheese sandwich with them in the field, but then returned to the house with *Dawdi* Zeke. The boy's shoulders had slumped with weariness, but Jakob was pleased with his efforts. He was learning to become a good, hardworking man.

Now, it was late afternoon and Jakob was anxious about Abby. He looked to where she sat on the bench of the planter, still driving the team. Her spine was stiff, her head held high, but her arms lagged. Pulling against those big horses all day was enough to make anyone's muscles ache. Throughout the day, he'd tried to help her refill the hoppers but was embarrassed when his leg gave out on him and he almost dropped a bag of seed on the ground. She'd saved him just in time, taking the heavy weight of the bag against her own slender body. Though she hadn't uttered one word of complaint, she must have been absolutely tuckered out. In spite of her determination, she didn't have the strength of a man. He hated to push her so hard, especially knowing how Simon had abused her. Jakob certainly couldn't fault her work. Not when they almost had all of the corn planted.

Correction. *Abby* almost had the corn planted. He'd done nothing but sit in the shade and watch her work. In spite of the long rest, his leg throbbed unbearably. And no wonder. A horrific black-and-red bruise surrounded his entire calf and extended down his ankle to his foot and up to his knee. No doubt the blood pooling was the cause of the swelling and pain. In spite of the cold compress *Mamm* had sent for him at noon, it would take time for the wound to heal.

If he and Abby could just make it through the evening milking, they could both rest. *Mamm* would undoubtedly have a hearty meal prepared for them, if they weren't too sick and tired to eat it. He longed to retire but wouldn't leave Abby's side as long as she stood out in the baking sun, doing his work.

"Hallo!"

Jakob turned. *Dawdi* Zeke was driving their smallest wagon toward the field with a stranger sitting beside him. Both men wore straw hats and black suspenders, so Jakob knew their guest was Amish.

Shading his eyes, he tried to discern who the stranger was. Then, he groaned.

Martin Hostetler.

No doubt the man was here to see Abby. Jakob should be glad that one of their faithful members was interested in her. His thoughts toward Martin were uncharitable. He shouldn't mind having the other man here, but he did.

Pursing his lips, Jakob waved to get Abby's attention. After a moment, she saw him and called to the team. When she noticed Zeke and Martin, she paused for a moment, then kept on going.

Hmm. That was an interesting reaction. Jakob wasn't certain if she recognized Martin and wanted to avoid him, or if she was simply eager to finish the last column of planting. A few more minutes and she'd be done.

"Look who came to visit," *Dawdi* Zeke said as he pulled up next to Jakob.

"*Hallo*, Martin." Jakob tugged on the brim of his hat, determined to be polite.

"Hi, Jakob." Martin's gaze riveted over to Abby. She'd turned the horses and was heading toward them, her head bowed slightly as she concentrated on holding the horses in a straight line.

With the giant Belgians as a backdrop, she looked so small and frail sitting on the planter. But Jakob had learned she had a strong will and fortitude. Abby was a survivor. A good woman who would stand beside a good man against the storms of life. Jakob just didn't think Martin was the right man for her.

"What brings you all the way out here?" Jakob asked.

"I heard you got hurt and wanted to see if you needed any help," Martin said.

The man scanned the vast field. The rows

weren't all perfectly straight, but they were planted and ready for growth. Since she was driving a strange team of horses, Jakob thought Abby had done an outstanding job and he couldn't have asked for more.

"As you can see, we've almost got the work done, thanks to Abby," he said.

"She's a strong little thing, isn't she?" Martin said, a wide smile on his face.

No, not really. At least, not physically. But Jakob didn't say that. Considering Abby's petite height and build, he didn't think she was strong at all. But her determination made up for a lot of what she lacked in physical stature.

"You could have asked me to plant your fields. It would have been easier on Abby," Martin said.

"*Ja*, but you have your own fields to plant," Jakob said.

Normally, Jakob would have contacted the bishop to see who in their district might be able to help out. The Amish assisted each other whenever there was trouble, but they had only nine families in their congregation. And honestly, Jakob didn't want Martin here, mainly because the man was interested in Abby. As far as Jakob was concerned, no one was good enough for Abby.

Wait a minute! Where had that thought come from? Jakob wasn't sure.

"I would have made the time. My *vadder* and I finished planting our fields five days ago. I could have helped you out," Martin insisted.

Hyperactivity came to Jakob's mind. He wasn't surprised that Martin had finished his planting days earlier. He just hoped their sprouting crops didn't get caught by a late freeze.

"*Danke* for the offer. We'll keep you in mind if we need help planting our hay," *Dawdi* Zeke said.

Jakob just nodded, forcing himself to smile. No one could accuse Martin of being lazy or unkind. The man was definitely a hard worker and an amazing horse trainer. One of the best in the state. He was Jakob's brother in the faith. It wasn't Christian for him to feel uncharitable toward the man. But he did. Which didn't make sense. He'd never had any problem with the man before…

Before Abby came. Too bad Martin had shown up just as they were finishing.

"She's an amazing woman, that's for sure. Some wise man should marry her while she's still eligible. It'd be a shame for her to leave us," *Dawdi* Zeke said.

Jakob jerked his head around and stared at his grandfather. He sensed that the elderly man was digging at him, to get him to propose to Abby. But he couldn't. Not if he wanted to remain loyal to Susan.

They talked for the next few minutes. Or rather, Martin and *Dawdi* Zeke talked. Jakob just listened and nodded when appropriate. And when Abby pulled the horses up, Martin waved both of his hands over his head. Other than a nod of the head, she paid him no heed and kept on going.

"Schtopp!" she called to the horses.

She'd reached the end of the column and raised the marking bar. She was finished, and Jakob breathed a long sigh of relief.

Still pulling the planter, the Belgians plodded over to the men. The horses had worked hard today and were undoubtedly eager for their comfortable stalls in the barn. They'd earned their supper tonight.

"Hallo, Martin," Abby said, her voice sounding unenthusiastic or tired, Jakob wasn't sure which. Maybe both.

"Hallo!" Martin smiled wide, his buoyant greeting making up for anything that Abby's lacked.

Her face looked pale against cheeks rosy from the sun. Now that her burden was over with, she hunched her shoulders and flexed her arms, as though they ached.

"I'm sorry I didn't stop right away. I knew if I did, I wouldn't feel up to finishing the field today. And it had to be done now," she said.

Again, a blaze of guilt speared Jakob's chest. He'd pushed her too hard today, but she'd been a stand-up woman. He'd counted on her and she hadn't let him down. Spunky and dedicated, just like Susan had been.

Thinking about his wife just then made him feel grouchy for some reason. He told himself it was because his leg was throbbing, but he knew it was something more. Something he didn't fully understand.

"I think I'll head back to the house," Jakob said.

"Me, too," *Dawdi* said. "Martin, why don't you ride back to the house with Abby? You can drive the Belgians and it'll give you two a chance to talk alone."

"*Ja*, I would like that." Martin eagerly hopped out of the small wagon and climbed up to sit beside Abby.

She readily handed over the lead lines to his capable hands, but she didn't look too eager to be alone with him. She stared at *Dawdi* as if he were abandoning her.

"See you back at the house," *Dawdi* said.

Jakob slapped the leads against the horse pulling his seed wagon. *Dawdi* followed behind.

Abby watched them go. Her gaze followed Jakob for just a moment, her eyes filled with some emotion he couldn't name. A pleading look he found both frustrating and endearing. He hated to leave her alone with Martin, but it couldn't be helped right now. She was a fully grown woman and would need to choose whom she married. If she wasn't interested in Martin, she would have to tell him so. Jakob had nothing to do with it. It was up to her.

When Jakob reached the main yard, he pulled the seed wagon up in front of the barn. *Dawdi* Zeke was right. Abby was amazing and should marry and raise a *familye* of her own. He'd thought that he was her protector. That he was doing a great service by keeping her safe. Yet, she'd done nothing but help him and his *familye* since she'd arrived. It wasn't right for Jakob to hold her back. He had to let her live her own life. And yet, he didn't want her to leave. Not ever. But how could he embrace her without being disloyal to Susan? Thinking about another woman made him feel like he was betraying his wife and the love they had shared, the children they'd had and the plans they'd made together.

No matter how he looked at the situation, he just couldn't see a way out. Not without losing Abby or Susan for good.

Chapter Ten

Abby slipped silently out of the bathroom. Dark shadows clogged the hallway, the moon gleaming through the window at the top of the stairs. The floorboards creaked beneath her bare feet and she paused, not wanting to disturb the sleeping children. It was late, but she'd been so grimy after planting the corn that she'd desperately needed to clean up.

Wearing a heavy bathrobe, she longed to crawl into bed and sleep for a zillion years. She couldn't remember being so tired. Even Martin Hostetler's incessant chatter at supper hadn't bothered her. He'd stayed rather late, sitting with her on the front porch and sipping a glass of lemonade as they listened to the chirp of crickets. She'd been too exhausted to participate much in the conversation, but she couldn't begrudge his presence. Not when he'd been such a huge help with the evening chores. He'd unhitched the draft horses and tossed them some hay while Abby ensured they had plenty of fresh water. Then he'd unloaded the unused bags of seed corn and stacked them in a tidy corner of the barn.

Jakob had hobbled out to the barn, intending to assist. His leg was so swollen that Naomi had been forced to slit the trouser leg up to the knee. All he could do was sit on a bench and gaze helplessly while she and Martin milked the cows. As she had worked, she'd felt Jakob watching her. A couple of times, she'd looked over at him, to assess his discomfort. The last thing she wanted was for him to collapse and have Martin help her get him back to the house.

He'd glanced away, seeming embarrassed to be caught staring. From the tense lines on his face, she could tell his injury was still hurting. No doubt he was relieved to have the work done. And she was so glad to be a part of that accomplishment. To make him pleased and reassured.

She hoped Martin wasn't too disappointed in her. She'd been exhausted. When he'd finally been ready to leave, she'd walked him to his buggy. Beneath the moonlit sky, he'd asked if he could court her. Feeling no attraction for him, she'd turned away and told him the truth. That they could never be more than friends.

"Someday, you'll find someone special," she'd said.

"I hope so." He'd shown a half smile but no malice as he turned and got into the buggy and drove away.

Now, Abby lit a bright lamp and set it on the tall chest beside her bed. She jerked the blankets back, not even caring if Reuben might have put cracker crumbs between her sheets. At this point, she was drained enough to sleep through a nuclear explosion. Just a few more minutes and she could close her eyes and rest.

Her body trembled like gelatin. Several times throughout the day, she'd feared the Belgians might pull her arms out of their sockets. For the most part, the horses were gentle beasts, but they were so strong. By late afternoon, it had taken every ounce of willpower to keep tension on the lead lines. It had taken a lot of exertion to direct the horses where she wanted them to go.

She laid her bathrobe on the foot of the bed. Dressed in her modest flannel nightgown, she pushed the sleeves down over her shoulders. Reaching for a pot of aloe vera cream she'd made herself, she popped the lid and kneaded the salve into her skin with slow, purposeful strokes. The ache was bittersweet. Though her muscles were stiff and sore, she felt a deep satisfaction for what she had completed. She'd earned Jakob's, Naomi's and *Dawdi* Zeke's respect. The seed corn was in the ground. Her efforts had been worth it. Tomorrow, she'd turn on the irrigation sprinklers in the morning and help Naomi with the baking in the afternoon. All would be well.

"Abby, are you still awake?"

She turned and gasped. Naomi stood peering around the slightly ajar door. The woman's eyes widened in surprise, and Abby didn't need to ask why. She scrambled to pull the sleeves of her nightgown back over her shoulders. With it settled into place, she faced Naomi.

"Abby! Those scars. What happened to you?" Naomi stepped into the room and reached to touch Abby's arm, but she drew away.

No, no! Naomi had seen what Abby had tried so hard to hide. Her cheeks flooded with heat. She didn't want anyone's pity. She felt ashamed, as if she'd done something wrong. Like she should run away. But she wouldn't do that ever again. She was a grown woman now and lived here in Colorado. She was safe. She didn't need to hide anymore.

Or did she?

"*Ach*, it's nothing," she said. "Just some old

scars from an accident years ago. I'd almost forgotten about them."

Or at least, she'd tried to forget. And to forgive. It was what *Gott* would want her to do after all. To let the atonement wash away her pain and grief. And her anger. Now that she was an adult, she was determined to be happy. To put the sad times behind her. She'd tried so hard to let go of her ire. It was only at moments like this that the past abuse she'd suffered still haunted her.

Brushing off her morose mood, Abby reached for her comb to part her hair down the middle. She smiled, acting like nothing was wrong. "I still can't believe we got the corn planted today."

"*Ja*, it was a big job. We are ever in your debt." Naomi stood beside the bed and folded her arms, her forehead crinkled in a frown of concern. "Land's sake, child. Those scars don't look like nothing to me. Are there more? I couldn't see your back. It looked like the scars went all the way down. What accident could have caused those horrible marks on your skin?"

So much for her attempt to distract Naomi. Shaking her head, Abby forced herself to concentrate on her hair. Fearing Naomi might see the agony written in her eyes, she refused to meet the older woman's gaze. "I fell, that's all. It's a bad memory I'd rather forget. Please let it go."

Naomi opened her mouth, as though she wanted to say more. She must have changed her mind, because she pursed her lips instead. "I'm worried about you, that's all. If anyone hurt you, they should be dealt with."

Abby turned and rested a hand on her arm. "What's done is done. *Gott* has taken care of me. There's no need to worry. I'm fine now. Really, I am."

The older woman continued to scowl, not looking convinced at all. Abby forced herself to relax. To think about the many blessings in her life. She didn't need to live in the past. Not anymore. She could be happy now and made a conscious choice to feel joy instead of fear and pain.

"Was there something you wanted to speak with me about?" Abby asked, trying to keep her tone light and not let her hands shake as she brushed out her long hair.

"*Ja*, but I can't remember what it was now. I guess I'm getting old and forgetful." Naomi gave a soft laugh and waved her hand in the air.

"*Ne*, you just have a lot on your mind. But I'll help you with the baking. I've got to figure out how to move the sprinkler system first.

Jakob said it's not difficult and he'll show me what to do."

"He's right. It's not hard at all. I've moved the sprinklers many times. If he keeps his leg elevated, he can ride out to the field in the wagon with you and coach you on what to do."

"Then all is well." Abby set the brush down and came to embrace the older woman.

Naomi hugged her back. "*Danke* for what you did today. You're such an asset to us. I'm so grateful you came to stay here."

Abby froze. The burn of tears caused her to blink several times. For a few moments, she felt overwhelmed by emotion. No one had ever said such wonderful words to her before.

"*Danke.* That's the nicest thing anyone's ever said to me," she whispered.

Naomi drew back and smiled tenderly before patting Abby's cheek. "I'm only speaking the truth. I don't know what we would do without you. Now, you rest."

The woman turned and left the room, closing the door softly behind her. Abby bit her bottom lip, sinking down onto the bed. She'd been so worried about coming here. Colorado was a different place. In Ohio, she'd never had to move heavy sprinkler pipes to water their crops. When she'd first arrived in Colorado, she'd been so worried that Jakob wouldn't remember her, or really want to marry her. Part of her fears had come true. There would be no wedding. Not for her. Which meant she had no permanent home. She didn't belong anywhere. Not really.

And then a thought occurred to her. What if Jakob found someone else to wed? Abby couldn't stay here if he took a new bride. He'd want his room back, so he could set up housekeeping with his wife. The children would have a new mother. The *familye* wouldn't need her any longer. She'd be in the way, like a sore thumb.

She'd have to leave eventually. But where could she go? Everyone in her faith expected her to marry. And if she did that, she would never be a free agent. Never in charge of her own happiness. But she believed it was what *Gott* expected. To raise her own *familye*.

Instead of pushing him away, maybe she should have encouraged Martin Hostetler more. He wasn't bad-looking. He was nice enough and a hard worker, but she could never bring herself to marry him. Not even to provide herself with a permanent home. In spite of Naomi's comforting words, Abby felt as though her situation here at the Fishers' farm was temporary. She couldn't stay here forever. Jakob could decide to marry someone else one day, and then she'd be in the way. She must find a ~~stable place to live. A place to belong forever.~~ And yet, leaving this farm scared Abby more than anything else she'd faced. Because now that she was here, she never wanted to go.

Nine days later, the swelling in Jakob's leg had gone down enough that he could walk without wincing. The bruise had faded to an ugly yellowish-brown, with the hoof print still outlined clearly across his flesh. The injury could have been so much worse. He'd been blessed and thanked *Gott* for taking care of him and for sending Abby to them.

As usual, he awoke early to do the morning chores. No matter how exhausted he was, his body clock always woke him up at the same time every day.

After washing and dressing, he opened the door to the *dawdy haus* and stepped outside. The night shadows embraced him. Joe nudged his leg with his black nose, and Jakob patted the dog's head. The animal accompanied him silently as he crossed the yard toward the barn. The early morning air wasn't as chilly as it had been a week ago, and he was satisfied that there would be no killing frost to destroy their crops. Any day now, the corn would begin to sprout. A feeling of anticipation swept over him. He couldn't wait to see the fields burgeoning with new growth, which would turn into tall green stalks. He had Abby to thank for their bounty.

As he passed the house, he wondered if she was up yet. Usually she beat him to the barn. A light glimmered in the upstairs bedroom where she was staying. That meant she was still inside, moving slower than usual. He hated to work her so hard. He dreaded the thought that she might think he was just as bad as Simon. If he could finish the milking before she arrived, it might alleviate her load today.

As he entered the barn, the prospect of being alone with Abby brought him a feeling of excitement. He had to remind himself that Martin Hostetler wanted to court her, even though she wasn't interested in the man. She didn't know it, but word had spread quickly of her polite rebuttal. Her lack of attraction both pleased and disappointed Jakob. Marriage would mean that she'd have to leave, and he didn't want her to go. His desires were purely selfish, and he was ashamed that he resented Martin. In the past couple of weeks, he'd grown too accustomed to Abby's presence here on the farm, yet she deserved so much more.

Inside the barn, the scent of animals and fresh straw filled his nose. He lit a lamp and tossed feed to the cows. While they munched contentedly, he set a milking stool beside one of the black-and-white Holsteins. Bucket in hand, he eased himself onto the stool and leaned his head against the animal's warm side as he began his morning ritual. He'd moved on to the second Holstein when Abby slipped into the barn.

"*Guder mariye*, Jakob," she said, her face glowing with a shy smile.

"Good morning, Abby. You slept late today," he said.

A glaze of doubt filled her eyes, and she twined her fingers together in front of her. He had learned that this was a nervous gesture she did whenever she feared retribution.

"I'm sorry. I… I'll get up earlier in the future," she said.

He snorted and spoke softly, so she would know he wasn't angry. "*Ach*, no need to fret. I think you could use a rest. No one can fault how hard you work."

Her tensed shoulders relaxed just a bit, and she retrieved a clean bucket and stool. Sitting beside the cream-colored Jersey, she started milking. The *whoosh-whoosh* sounds of the milk spraying into the buckets had a calming effect, and they didn't speak for several minutes.

"Are you helping *Mamm* bake pies today?"

he finally asked, knowing tomorrow was Friday and bakery day.

"*Ja*, and a strawberry swirl sheet cake with white icing. Sarah Yoder said it's a special order. One of the *Englischers* wants it for their daughter's birthday party tomorrow evening. Naomi is going to decorate it with clouds and balloons. It'll bring in double the normal price."

Not that it would cost the *Englischer* a lot. They charged only what was fair, never allowing greed to enter into the equation. That was one reason the bakery was so popular among the *Englisch*. Their prices were so reasonable.

"*Gut.*" He chuckled, then paused before broaching the question on his mind. "Abby, I'm sorry to pry, but there's something I'd like to ask you. It's rather personal."

"What do you want to know?" she asked.

She kept milking, barely looking up…a sure sign that she wasn't as skittish around him anymore. In fact, he thought they were becoming good friends.

He took a deep inhale, remembering what Naomi had told him several days earlier. Even now, he still felt furious and tried to remember that *Gott* expected him to be patient and kind no matter what. "Did Simon or your father beat you with a whip or a strap?"

She jerked, so suddenly that the Jersey cow

shifted her weight restlessly and swung her large head around to look at Abby with round, dark eyes.

Abby stared into her bucket, her bent head appearing so sad and forlorn. At first, Jakob thought she was still milking, but he couldn't hear the *whooshing* sounds anymore. He'd upset her with his question, but he had to know. He resisted the urge to stand and take her into his arms and comfort her.

"Why…why do you ask?" she said, her voice sounding small.

He shrugged. "*Mamm* mentioned that she'd seen some old scars on your shoulders. You told her they were from an accident, but she said the marks looked like someone had whipped you. She's just worried about you. So am I."

There. He'd admitted it to her. No taking it back. And yet, the confession came so easily, which surprised him. He told himself that he cared about this woman the way he cared about all of *Gott's* children. That was all. And yet, he knew what he felt for Abby was a bit more than that.

"It's over and done with. I'd rather not discuss it now," she whispered.

So. Maybe they weren't as good friends as he had hoped. But her response answered his question well enough, although he still didn't know what had happened, or if it had been her father or Simon who had beaten her. And though it no longer mattered, he wished she would confide in him. He sensed that bottling up what had happened inside herself would prevent her from healing fully. She needed to let it out. To talk about it with someone who cared. He was just glad that she was far away from the people who had once abused her. All Amish tried to follow the Savior's loving example by shunning acts of violence. For this reason, he didn't understand how Simon could be so cruel to his sister yet still call himself a man of faith.

She returned to her milking, ignoring their conversation. From his angle, he could see the backs of her arms flexing rhythmically as she milked the cow.

"Are you going to the singing with Martin on Sunday evening?" Jakob purposefully changed the discussion by addressing another uncomfortable topic that was weighing heavily on his mind.

She missed a beat in her milking, and the Jersey stomped a foot in agitation. "I… I don't think so."

He hesitated, wondering what he should say. A part of him knew it wasn't good for her to hide out here on the farm. She should mingle with others of their faith. But another part of him didn't want her to socialize with other men. He was being selfish again.

"I don't want to interfere, but Martin is a *gut* man. You should go with him," he said, forcing himself to be magnanimous.

"He…he comes on a bit too strong for me," she said.

"*Ja*, but he means well. You always know where you stand with Martin. He is strong in his faith and would be a good provider to whomever he marries. The more time you spend with him, the more you'll get used to him."

She looked over her shoulder at him with a doubtful glint in her eyes. He didn't want her to leave anytime soon, but her welfare and happiness meant more to him than his own self-seeking desires.

"I've already told him I'm not interested in being anything more than friends," she said, turning back to her work.

The Jersey jostled against her and gave a mournful *moo*, as though eager to be finished with this chore. Abby patted the cow's side in a reassuring gesture.

"That is too bad. You're young and should have some fun. You won't know if you really like him unless you go with him more," he suggested.

"I… I'd rather not."

Jakob read between the lines. Abby didn't trust men and feared Martin might be assertive like her father and brother.

"If it helps, I have never heard anything bad spoken about Martin or his *familye*. His *mudder* and sisters always seem so happy that I don't believe he or his *vadder* treat them unkindly," Jakob said.

Abby looked up, her eyes wide and filled with suffering and angst. Then it was gone and she smiled, hiding her inner feelings. But he knew the truth and longed to comfort her. To tell her she was safe now. But the moment she left his home, he would no longer be able to protect her. And that's when he realized he didn't know much about Martin Hostetler either. Not really. Martin had come from Indiana. Jakob's *familye* had not known the Hostetlers before they moved to Colorado six years earlier. He thought they were good people, but how could he really know what went on inside the walls of their home when no one was watching? It would require a leap of faith on Abby's part.

"I'd rather take it slow. I may never marry at all," she said, her voice sounding noncommittal.

He jerked his head up, blinking at her in

surprise. Not marry? Ever? The idea was alien to him.

"You should marry. It is what *Gott* would want."

"I know you really believe that. I do, too. Or at least, I used to. I'm not so sure anymore."

Hmm, he didn't like the sound of that. No doubt she felt that way because of him. She'd come all the way to Colorado, thinking he would become her husband. She didn't seem to want Martin or any man, which left her with few options. But marriage was a way of life to the Amish. *Familye* was everything to them. Jakob couldn't accept anything different. And yet, how could he fault Abby when he was shunning marriage for himself?

"Of course you will marry one day. Until that time, you have a home here for as long as you want it," he said.

Again, she showed a doubtful frown, but didn't say anything. The Jersey gave a low bellow and lashed out with her back hoof, striking Abby against the shoulder. The woman cried out and toppled over her stool, lying on her back on the hard-packed ground.

"Abby!"

Jakob scrambled off his stool and crouched over her. She groaned, reaching to clutch her injured shoulder. She breathed hard, her eyes closed.

"Are you okay?" he asked, grateful the cow hadn't struck Abby's head.

She nodded and opened her eyes, rubbing her shoulder. Gazing up at him, she released a whimsical laugh. "You and I make quite a pair. We keep getting kicked by the livestock. At this rate, we'll both be black-and-blue before long. Bishop Yoder will wonder what's going on here at this farm."

He chuckled, enjoying her sense of humor. Considering her past, it was good that she could laugh about the situation. The flash of worry he'd felt had left him shaking. He didn't want to worry about this woman. Didn't want to care.

But he did.

Leaning over her, he pulled several pieces of straw away from her white *kapp*. Her wide blue eyes met his, and he felt lost in their depths. Captivated. Drawn closer until he kissed her, a gentle caress that deepened for several moments. She lifted a hand to rest against his chest, just over his heart. He breathed her in, then remembered who he was and who she was and that she was not Susan. He jerked back, his face heating up with embarrassment. They gazed into one another's eyes with startled wonder. And Jakob felt a new awareness sweep over him. Abby wasn't just a girl from his past. She was now a beautiful woman.

"Jakob," she said his name, so softly that he almost didn't hear her.

Reality crashed over him and he felt awful for what he'd done, as if he'd taken advantage of her. "I… I'm sorry, Abby."

He hurried to his feet and helped her stand, then moved away and folded his arms. He couldn't meet her gaze. Couldn't face the disloyalty he felt toward his wife. He'd taken vows with Susan. He'd promised to love her until the day he died. Never once had he been tempted by another woman.

Until now.

"That was wrong of me. A lapse in judgment. It won't happen again," he said.

He bent over and picked up his milk bucket, eager to give his hands something to do. Abby was overly quiet, and he wondered what she was thinking. He already knew she didn't trust men, and he'd just given her a reason not to trust him.

"Is your shoulder all right? Maybe we should ask *Mamm* to put a cold pack on it for you," he said, trying to ease his guilt.

She nodded, looking flushed and embarrassed as she moved her shoulder carefully to test its soundness. "It's fine. I suppose I'll have a bruise, but it'll be all right."

A long, dark silence followed as they gathered up the milk pails and headed toward the house. They didn't speak, didn't acknowledge what had transpired between them. Jakob thought that was best. But no matter how hard he tried, he couldn't forget what had happened. Nor could he deny that he had feelings for Abby. He was definitely attracted to her, but that wasn't enough. Not for him, and not for her. Because deep in his heart, he didn't believe he could ever love her the way he loved Susan. And after everything Abby had been through, she deserved for someone to adore her. But that someone couldn't be him.

Chapter Eleven

Abby took a deep inhale of fresh air before tucking a strand of hair back inside her *kapp*. Gazing at the wide-open sky, she squinted at the noonday sun, enjoying its warmth on her face. A couple of weeks had passed since Jakob had kissed her in the barn. A couple of weeks that made her feel jittery every time he was near. They hadn't spoken about the incident since then, and she thought perhaps she'd imagined it ever happened. Now, she wished that she could forget.

Soft clods of dirt broke beneath her feet as she walked along one wide furrow of the cornfield. Shifting the wicker basket she carried to her other hand, she thought about Jakob's and Reuben's lunches tucked inside. Later that afternoon, she would plant tomatoes. Hopefully she would have lots of beans, peas and corn to put up in bottles in August.

A mild breeze ruffled the green sprouts growing in long rows of the fertile field. Like any farmer, seeing the verdant color of the new plants brought Abby a deep sense of joy and satisfaction. She paused a moment, waiting for Ruby to catch up. The girl hopped over several rows, then came running in her bare feet. The edge of her purple pinafore apron rippled in the wind.

"There's *Daed* and Reuben." Ruby pointed toward the south corner where Grape Creek bordered the fields. Clutches of purple wild iris grew along the banks.

Jakob's father had been wise to buy this farm. It came with deeded water rights and spring-fed water for the livestock. The creek twined its way across their property. Very handy for watering their garden and front lawn.

Correction. This was Jakob's property. Funny how she felt as though she belonged here, because she didn't. Not really. And yet, Abby had done so much work here that she couldn't help loving this land and caring about the *familye* that lived here.

She followed the long row to the end, conscious of Ruby skipping behind. Skirting the edge, she couldn't help noticing Jakob. And without a word being said, her cheeks flushed with heat as she again remembered the brief kiss they'd shared.

No! She shook her head, refusing to think of what had happened that day. It would only make her long for things that never could be.

Dressed in gray broad fall trousers, a blue shirt, suspenders and work boots, Jakob straddled the irrigation gate. His head was bowed as he scooped mud, sticks and grass out of the creek with a shovel. He slopped the black muck against the outer bank, then dug out some more. No doubt the irrigation ditch was clogged.

Back east, they had much more rainfall to sustain their crops. But here in the West, there was a reason they called the life-sustaining water "liquid gold." Without it, Jakob's fields would dry up to dust.

If all went well, they would harvest the corn in the fall. And then the wedding season would begin. Abby dreaded it. She'd come to Colorado planning to marry. Though she was determined to carry on, she couldn't help feeling slightly disillusioned. Okay, more than slightly. If she were honest with herself, it had been a huge disappointment.

"Now?" She heard Reuben ask. Neither he nor Jakob were aware that Abby and Ruby had arrived with their noon meal.

"*Ja*, let it go." Jakob stood back and nodded, looping his free hand around one of his suspenders.

The boy grunted as he tugged on the metal gate. It finally gave with a low grating sound. A rush of water sped past them, soon filling the small ditch. Tossing his shovel onto the opposite bank, Jakob reached for a hoe and directed the water down a number of corn rows. The cracked earth greedily soaked up the moisture as it sped forward along the furrow.

Abby watched in fascination. On her brother's farm in Ohio, they'd used gravity irrigation for the garden and pivot sprinklers for their soybean crops, but they didn't have to water nearly as often as they did here in the West. At supper last night, Jakob had indicated it would take hours each day for him to water their thirsty crops. And Abby knew an inch of water could make all the difference in doubling their production versus reaping just enough to barely subsist on.

"*Daed*, we brought your food," Ruby called in a cheerful voice.

Jakob looked up as he pulled several weeds out of the ground and smiled at his daughter. "And just in time, too. I'm ravenous."

"Me, too," Reuben said. He smiled at his sister, but the disapproving frown slid into place when he glanced at Abby.

Jakob's gaze shifted to Abby, and she looked away, feeling suddenly flushed with heat. He removed his straw hat and wiped his forearm across his forehead. Abby stood next to him, trying not to notice how his slightly damp hair curled against the back of his neck.

"The crops seem to be doing well. Every row has sprouted," she said. Which meant she had planted the seed properly.

He nodded, a smile curving his handsome mouth. "*Ja*, and I'm finding very few insects that will harm the corn. We should have a bumper crop this year, but I may need to use an herbicide next year to keep the weeds down."

To emphasize his point, he gave a jerk of his hand, pulling another weed out by the roots before tossing it aside.

"After I've planted the garden today, I can help weed," she offered.

"I'll help *Daed* with the weeding," Reuben said, his jaw hard as he lifted it slightly higher.

"I'm sure you're a big help to your *vadder*," she said, trying not to rile the youngster. She still felt bad that her mere presence seemed to rankle the boy so much.

"I think there are enough weeds for all of us to pull." Jakob chuckled and tossed another one aside where its roots would dry up in the sunshine. "Let's sit down." He gestured toward the bank by the creek.

Ruby took the basket from Abby and plopped down before opening the lid. "Wait until you see what we brought you."

She pulled out a cloth and laid it across the coarse grass, then removed several plastic containers. She grunted as she popped the lid of one and held the dish up for inspection.

"Chocolate cream pie. Yum!" Reuben said.

"*Ja*, Abby made it and I helped."

At the mention of Abby's name, Reuben scowled and looked away. Abby didn't understand. Sometimes the boy would smile at her, then seem to catch himself and frown instead. During meals or as they were working around the farm. Almost as though he were fighting against himself and purposefully trying not to like her.

"You helped?" Jakob looked pleasantly surprised.

"She did. I couldn't have done it without her," Abby said, noticing how the girl beamed.

"That's nice. No doubt you'll be as good a cook as Abby and *Grossmammi* one day." Jakob's voice was filled with complimentary thanks.

"*Ja*, it was easy. Just mix a box of pudding.

But Abby also adds cream for more richness. She taught me how," Ruby said.

Abby sat near Reuben, hiding a smile of amusement. Ruby had quoted her words verbatim, speaking as if she now knew a special secret. But honestly, it had been fun to teach the girl to make a cream pie. Even Naomi had watched with a critical eye as Abby had stirred in the cream. The older woman had then commented that it was a clever way to add in a richer flavor to the pudding mix.

"The pie is for after lunch. First, we should eat something more nutritious." Abby reached into the basket, then handed each of the boys a ham-and-cheese sandwich.

Reuben peeled back the wrapper, and a small slip of paper fell out. Although the children were now out of school for the summer, over the past weeks, Abby had continued putting uplifting notes in his lunch. She also left a special message around the house for Ruby to find each day. While Ruby was delighted by the kind messages, Reuben continued to deny ever receiving them.

The boy picked up the note and Abby held her breath, thinking he might finally read and comment on it. Instead, he crumpled it in his fist and let it fall to the ground. Jakob and Ruby were busy with their own food and didn't seem to notice.

Abby's heart plummeted. She released a low sigh of frustration, thinking she might never win the boy's approval.

Sitting beside her brother, Ruby plunged her bare feet into the cooling water of the creek. Reuben soon thrust his feet in, too. Between bites of her own sandwich, Ruby chattered nonstop about how tall the corn sprouts were getting and how big the kittens were growing. Since he loved both topics as much as the girl did, Reuben didn't seem to mind her constant babbling.

"We're gonna have a bumper crop of corn, that's for sure," Reuben said, quoting *Dawdi* Zeke.

"We're gonna have a bumper crop of kittens, too," Ruby said.

Reuben munched on some potato chips before tossing a few blades of grass into the swirling creek. "*Ja*, I think Tiger is the biggest."

"That's because he's a boy," Ruby said. "*Grossmammi* says the babies will soon be big enough to live in the barn, but I'd rather they lived in the house with us."

Taking a bite of food, Abby covered a low chuckle.

"Why do you think that's funny?" Jakob

whispered, leaning toward her with a conspiratorial glance.

Abby spoke in a quiet voice so Ruby wouldn't hear. "I think Naomi is tired of the kittens running around the kitchen and making messes. They've gotten big enough to climb out of their box and are constantly underfoot. Soon, they'll be all over the house. She is definitely ready for them to live in the barn."

He released a low laugh, then nodded and spoke loud enough for Ruby to hear. "Once they are old enough, the babies will live in the barn."

Ruby frowned over her shoulder at her father. "But I don't want them to get hit by a car like Amber. I want them to stay inside with us, where they will be safe."

Although Reuben was silent, his eyes also showed a glint of concern.

"We can't lock them up forever. Animals need to be free to live their life and be happy. Imagine how you would feel if I locked you in the house all day and night," Jakob said, his voice gentle but firm.

"I wouldn't like that at all," Ruby said.

"Neither would I," Reuben said.

"But *Daed*, they might get hurt if they live out in the barn..." Ruby spoke in a slightly whining voice.

"The cats will live in the barn. *Gott* will look after them, just as He looks after us," Jakob said, his tone hinting that there would be no more discussion on the subject.

As Abby expected, Reuben refused to eat the pie she'd made. Ruby had no such inhibitions and chewed with relish. Reuben glanced at her several times, a look of hunger in his eyes, but he didn't ask for any. Both children seemed overly quiet. Abby figured out why when she heard Ruby whisper to her brother.

"Do you really think *Gott* will protect the kittens if they live in the barn?"

"*Ja, Daed* said so and that's *gut* enough for me. Stop worrying about them," Reuben said.

Abby was impressed. Although Reuben hadn't seemed to accept his mother's death and he kept his distance from her, she knew the boy had a tender heart and trusted his father enough to accept his faith in the Lord. Even without their mother's aid, Jakob was doing a good job raising his children.

Ruby seemed to be rather gloomy now, fretting over the babies. Seeing her downcast expression, Reuben suddenly kicked his foot, splashing water on her.

"Hey!" Ruby kicked back and the two children were soon engaged in a water fight. With the heat of the day, it didn't matter. The water would cool them off.

"You can't catch me." Ruby hopped up and took off toward the corrals.

"*Ja*, I can." Reuben chased after her.

Their laughter filled the air as they let off some energy before returning to their chores.

Abby glanced over to where Reuben had dropped the note she had tucked into his sandwich, but it was no longer there. She shrugged, thinking it must have blown away.

Watching the children run, she smiled at their gaiety. "I wish Simon had played with me like that when we were young."

The moment she said the words, she regretted them. Jakob turned her way, having heard her comment. She'd tried to keep her past life private and didn't want to reveal more than she must. But Jakob already knew almost everything, so it didn't really matter anymore.

"Why do you think he wouldn't play with you?" Jakob asked.

She shrugged. "I fear he learned very early from our father to…"

She bit her tongue, trying not to speak the words.

"What did Simon learn from your father?" Jakob pressed, his voice soft but insistent.

Abby tucked the empty food containers back

into the basket. "You already know my *vadder* could be quite cruel at times."

Most of the time, actually. She had not one single memory of him ever smiling, and she had no idea what his laughter sounded like. In retrospect, she realized he must have been a very unhappy person. And Simon was just like him. She just didn't understand why. What had made her father so miserable?

Jakob rested a hand on her arm, and she went very still. "Abby. Please talk to me."

She lifted her head, meeting his gaze. He held a purple wild iris in front of her eyes. He'd plucked it from nearby. Abby stared, charmed by his gesture. It was the first time a man—any man—had given her a flower, and she wanted the moment to last. Taking it from him, she brought the velvety petals close to her face and breathed in their sweet fragrance.

"Don't you think Simon came up with some of his meanness on his own? He didn't learn it all from your *vadder*," Jakob said.

She caught the note of disapproval in his tone and hesitated before bowing her head. "I think all of us have the capacity for good and bad, but my *vadder* encouraged Simon through his poor example. You would never allow Reuben to treat Ruby badly. But you've also provided a good example for your children to follow. ~~Simon never had that in our home growing up.~~"

"*Danke* for the compliment. I try to be a good, responsible parent, although sometimes I need to do better. But I can't imagine ever whipping someone with a strap, even if I had seen my *vadder* do it. *Gott* would not approve of such actions. Not ever. Is that what your *vadder* did to you? Or is Simon responsible for the scars my *mudder* saw on your shoulders?" A bit of outrage tainted his questions.

Abby couldn't imagine whipping someone either, and yet it had happened to her. But it was still difficult to open up and tell him.

"I wish you'd confide in me. It might help," Jakob said, his voice soft with encouragement.

She hesitated as memories rushed over her. Normally, she would have said no. But this time, something felt different. Like she finally had a friend she could trust. Someone she could count on, who would never betray her.

She took a deep breath, thinking he might be right. For so long, she'd kept the abuse to herself, locked up inside her heart and mind. For years, she'd even blamed herself. But as she'd grown older and attended church, listening to the preachings, she'd learned that *Gott* didn't approve of such violence and anger. He was a kind, loving Heavenly Father who wanted only the best for His children.

For her.

In all these long years, she hadn't spoken about what had happened to anyone. Until now.

Before she could stop herself, it all poured out. Like a valve that had suddenly burst and the steam released in a hurried rush. Her voice wobbled, and she felt the burn of tears. She also felt the anger, the humiliation and the pain that followed. She told Jakob everything. About the whippings, the criticism and being locked in the root cellar when she was bad. Which must have been often, because she'd spent a lot of time in that dark place. She'd felt worthless and ugly inside. And when she finished her story, she stared at the wild iris lying in her lap, letting its beauty remind her that there was still so much to live for. Her hands were shaking, and she gripped them together to stop.

A long pause followed, with just the rustling of the wind to break the silence.

"You know *Gott* would never approve of what your *vadder* and Simon did to you, don't you?" Jakob asked.

No, for a long time, she'd really believed it was her fault. That if she worked harder and was smarter, faster, better, then her father would finally appreciate and love her. Now, she realized that Jakob was right. Her father's failing had nothing to do with her. At the time, spilling the milk had seemed so serious. So negligent. She'd felt horrible for what she'd done. Thoughtless and useless. But what about the times when she'd simply walked into a room and become the target of abuse? And for the umpteenth time, she wondered why her father had always gotten so upset at her. Why had he seemed to hate her so much? She would probably never know.

She took a deep inhale and let it go. "Perhaps *Gott* wanted me to learn from my experience. It has made me a much more compassionate person. For a long time, I thought I could make my *vadder* and Simon love me. But no matter how hard I tried, they always seemed to despise me. Especially Simon."

"He may not be capable of love," Jakob said, his voice filled with pity.

"*Ja*, and I think it must be because he hates himself. I wish I could have helped him somehow. To make him see how his hatred was cankering him inside and making him and everyone around him so unhappy. But he never allowed me to get close enough to try. I feel so sorry for his wife and *kinder*, because he has turned his anger on them, too." She wiped her damp eyes.

Jakob took her trembling hands into his and

squeezed gently, holding them for several moments. "Just as you said, we all have the capacity for good and bad. Simon is in control of his own actions, no matter what your *vadder* did. Instead of protecting and loving you, he made the choice to hurt you. He could have chosen differently. We each have our own free agency to choose."

Abby lifted her face and met his eyes. "*Ja*, you are right. But I can't help wondering. Wasn't I worthy of his protection? Wasn't I good enough to earn his and my *vadder's* love?"

"Oh, Abby." He took her into his arms and held her close.

She knew she shouldn't let him touch her. That she should push him away. But she couldn't do it. Instead, she breathed him in, feeling his warmth surrounding her. His protection. She felt so safe whenever he was near.

Finally, she moved back, feeling hollow inside. He'd been kind, but he loved Susan. They were friends and nothing more. It would be better if she just kept her distance and looked for a new place to live. She couldn't compete with a dead woman for his affections. She could never win his love. And that's what hurt most of all.

Jakob sat back and watched as Abby quickly packed up the basket. She carefully placed the wild iris he'd given her inside, and he wondered if she intended to keep it. He stood, thinking he should help her, but he didn't dare touch her again. He'd listened as she'd told him about her life, her voice an aching whisper. Tears had washed her cheeks, and he'd longed to brush them aside. To ease her pain and see her smile again. But he feared she might take his actions the wrong way. A feeling of love for Abby enveloped his being, but he fought it off. Even though she was gone, he couldn't betray his vows to Susan.

"You are worthy, Abby. You are a daughter of *Gott*. What could be more worthy than that?" he said, hoping she believed him.

She showed an unsteady smile. "*Danke* for listening to a foolish young woman's ramblings. But I'd appreciate it if you'd keep these things just between the two of us."

Her voice cracked and so did his heart.

Of course she didn't want others to know what had happened to her. He couldn't blame her. But he wished there was some way for her to see herself as he saw her. As a lovely woman who was worthy of a man's love. Not because of anything she did or didn't do, but simply because of who she was. If he hadn't already met Susan and given his heart away, he would be free to love Abby...

No! It did no good to think that way. He had married Susan. He had loved her. He always would. In the short time they'd been together, they had shared so much. A love like that didn't come along twice in a lifetime.

Or did it?

The outline of Abby's *kapp* and sweet profile looked so innocent that he longed to hold her in his arms again. But that would only increase the confusion between them. They were merely friends. It was best if he kept his distance, for both of their benefit.

"You are *willkomm*. And trust that I will not share your words with anyone, this I promise," he said.

A long, swelling silence followed.

She gestured to the bubbling creek. "Do you think we'll have enough water to last the summer?"

"*Ach*, I do. Someday when I've saved enough, I hope to buy a lateral irrigation system. It's expensive, but worth it. A pivot system is easier, but it wastes a lot of good land. A lateral system would cover the entire area of our rectangular fields and give us a much greater yield of produce." He spread his arms wide to indicate the corn and hay fields. "A sprinkler system would make it so that I could devote more time to our furniture-making business. I love farming, but I love working with the wood, too. I really think I could set up a shop and make a go of it in town, as long as I knew my *familye* had its needs met first."

"That plan sounds *wundervoll*. I have no doubt we can make it work."

She shifted her weight, and he sensed that she was restless. Then he realized that he'd just confided his own hopes and dreams to her, too. She was so easy to talk to. So easy to be around.

Glancing toward the house, he saw Reuben trotting toward them. The boy seemed to know that it was time to return to their labors. Ruby must have stayed at the house with Naomi.

"*Ach*, here comes Reuben. I better get back to work," he said.

"*Ja*, me, too. Naomi will be wondering what happened to me."

She stepped away and he watched her go. Ducking his head, he picked up his hoe and started working with the water, weeding as he moved down each row. He longed to call her back, to ask if she could help with the weeding. They could visit while they worked together and make the chore pass more quickly. The thistle and lamb's-quarter were bad this year. If he didn't remain vigilant, the weeds could crowd out the corn and cause yield loss in their crop.

When he looked up, Reuben stood in another row, hoeing out the weeds. Abby was gone. No doubt she was inside the house, helping *Mamm* with the baking, washing laundry, scrubbing floors or tending to the kittens.

"Why don't you like Abby?" he asked his son.

Reuben jerked his head up, a surprised look on his face. "I… I just don't."

Jakob leaned against the handle of his hoe, choosing his words carefully. "She's done nothing to hurt you."

"I know." Reuben looked away, a guilty flush staining his face.

"Then why are you so sharp with her? Why won't you eat any of the delicious pies she makes?"

"*Mamm* made pies, too," the boy said.

Ah, yes. And no doubt the youngster thought no one could make pies as well as his mother.

"Is that it? You think Abby is trying to take your *mudder's* place?" Jakob asked.

The boy gave a belligerent jerk of his shoulders. "I don't know."

Jakob stepped across the row and placed two fingers beneath the boy's chin before lifting his head to meet his eyes. "*Mein sohn*, you have been given a great gift. You remember your ~~mudder so well. You know how much she loved~~ you and you loved her. Don't you?"

Reuben answered fiercely, his eyes suddenly damp. "*Ja*, she loved me and I loved her."

"And no one can ever take that love from you. But Abby never really knew her *mudder*. She has lived her entire life believing that no one loves her."

The boy's brow crinkled. "What about her *vadder* and *bruder*?"

Jakob shook his head sadly. "Not even them."

"But why? Your *familye* is s'posed to love you no matter what."

How innocent his son was. How sweet, loyal and impressionable. But Jakob was unwilling to betray Abby's confidence.

"It doesn't matter why. Until she marries, she only has us. I'm positive if she had lived, *Mamm* would have been good friends with Abby. She doesn't want to take your *mudder's* place. She just wants to live and be happy and accepted. It's okay for you to be nice and like her. Can you do that?"

The scowl remained firmly on Reuben's face, but his eyes filled with uncertainty. Jakob could tell the boy wanted to agree, but something held him back. A deep loyalty to his mother's memory. Jakob didn't want to force Reuben to comply. That would only lead to resentment and hate. The Savior always remained calm. He showed respect and taught truth, letting people decide for themselves if they would follow Him. Jakob would rather win his son's compliance through gentle persuasion and a genuine desire to do what was right.

"Think about it," Jakob said. "The Lord taught us to be fair and just. To be kind and loving. I know you will come to the right decision."

He returned to his work, leaving Reuben to consider his words. And that's when a thought occurred to Jakob. He was such a hypocrite. He told his son that it was okay to like Abby. That she couldn't take his mother's place. And yet, Jakob couldn't seem to accept his own advice. He'd been kind to Abby, but he didn't want to get close to her. Because doing so made him feel disloyal to Susan. But recognizing this flaw didn't make it any easier for Jakob to change how he felt. He couldn't love more than one woman. He just couldn't.

He thought about Abby leaving one day, and an immediate melancholy gripped his heart. She'd come to his *familye* at the worst possible time in their lives, after they'd lost two key members of their *familye*. In spite of that, his children seemed happier with her here.

Regardless of his stubborn insistence not to like her, even Reuben was calmer. Their farm was prospering during a time when his injury could have forced them to sell their land. With Abby's help, Naomi didn't look as exhausted all the time. And because he didn't have to do the heavy work, *Dawdi* Zeke's back pain had finally eased. Jakob knew they had Abby to thank. She had done the work of two. They would definitely all feel the loss if and when she finally left.

Chapter Twelve

The following week, Abby was outside taking clothes off the line when the rattle of a horse and buggy caused her to turn. Lizzie Beiler waved, the strings of her white *kapp* blowing in the wind.

"Guder daag," Lizzie called.

"Guder mariye," Abby returned, surprised to see her friend all the way out here.

Abby dropped a clean bath towel she had just folded into the laundry basket and walked out to meet Lizzie. She glanced up, noticing a cluster of gray storm clouds congregated just overhead. They might open up and rain by afternoon, but she'd have the laundry gathered in before then.

"What brings you all the way out to our farm?" Abby asked in a pleasant tone once Lizzie had stepped out of the buggy.

"I wanted to visit, so I brought you an apple cake." Lizzie reached inside the buggy and lifted out a basket covered with a clean white cloth.

"*Ach*, that's kind of you."

"Has Jakob recovered from his injury?" Lizzie asked.

"Almost. He's doing fine now. Come inside and I'll make you a cup of herbal tea."

Abby linked her arm with Lizzie's as they walked toward the house. A light breeze brushed past them, causing several leaves to scatter across the front yard.

"I also must confess I wanted to see how you are doing." Lizzie cast her a sideways glance.

"I'm fine, all things considered," Abby said.

"Any good news to report between you and Jakob?" Lizzie spoke low.

Abby didn't pretend not to understand. "*Ne*, there will be no wedding for Jakob and me, if that's what you mean."

Lizzie shrugged. "I won't give up hope yet. You two are ideal for each other."

Abby hid an inward sigh. "I'm afraid he is still mourning his wife, and I can't fault him for that. But honestly, I've been too busy to think much about it."

Which was partly true. The thought that she would never marry was rarely far from her mind, but she couldn't do anything about it, so she pushed it aside.

"And what about you? Have you heard from Eli yet?"

Lizzie shook her head. "*Ne*, and I don't expect to. He's been gone so long, I'm sure he's forgotten about me and moved on with his life."

Abby felt disheartened by this news. Both she and Lizzie had loved men who didn't want them. It was a sad state of affairs.

They stepped inside, where they were greeted warmly by Naomi. Soon, they were all gathered around the kitchen table, laughing and enjoying cups of peppermint tea and slices of Lizzie's apple cake. They saved a slice for Reuben and the two men, who were out in the barn mending the leather harness. With little Ruby listening in, Abby was grateful they could talk only about general topics. She feared if Lizzie pressed her much more, she might burst into tears and confide all her fears and broken dreams to the woman. Although it felt good to have a friend who cared about her, she was kind of relieved when Lizzie left a half hour later.

As Abby walked Lizzie outside to her buggy, she didn't mind when the other woman squeezed her hand. "If you need to talk, I'm always willing to listen. Take care of yourself."

"*Danke*, I will. And you, too. *Mach's gut.*" Abby tried to smile, but inside she started trembling. She didn't understand why thinking about Jakob and her dashed plans of having a *familye* of her own should bother her so much, but it did.

Resolved to exercise more faith in *Gott*, she waved as Lizzie drove away. Then she picked up the wicker basket filled with clean clothes and carried it upstairs to the children's room. After setting it on the floor, she slid open Reuben's top dresser drawer. She stared at the melee of clothing strewn around inside. What a mess! It looked like an eggbeater had been in here.

Shaking her head, she started folding each item into tidy piles. She laughed to herself, thinking that kids could be so chaotic. She'd spent a large part of the morning mending the *familye's* garments and wanted to get everything put away before Reuben caught her in his room. If he knew she'd darned his socks and mended his torn shirt, she feared he might refuse to wear them.

Bending at the waist, she lifted the repaired clothing and tucked it into the drawer. To make more room, she pushed the other clothing aside...then paused. A flash of white caught her eye. She reached to the farthest back corner of the drawer, and a pile of papers wrapped with a rubber band crackled as she pulled it forward.

Her notes! The uplifting messages she'd written and put in Reuben's lunch over the past weeks since she'd arrived. But what were they doing here?

She gaped in confusion, remembering all the times he'd denied receiving them. Even the note he'd thrown on the ground the day she'd confided in Jakob was here, spread carefully as if to remove the wrinkles from when he'd crumpled the paper in his fist. The wind hadn't blown it away after all. Reuben must have picked it up and kept it. Which meant that throwing it on the ground was all for show. But why? He'd made it clear that he disliked her. That he wanted nothing to do with her. So, why had he kept her notes?

"What are you doing in my stuff?"

She whirled around and found Reuben standing in the doorway. Dressed in his plain trousers, shirt and suspenders, he looked like a smaller replica of his father. His gaze took in the open drawer and the slips of paper she still clutched in one hand. And like a giant storm cloud moving across the sky, his face darkened.

"Those are mine. You have no right to go through my things!" he yelled, his cheeks flushing with embarrassment and anger.

Before she could explain, he rushed at her, knocking her backward. She cried out, her hands clawing at something, anything, to stop her fall. In the process, she dropped the papers. They rustled to the floor as she bounced against Ruby's bed. Reuben gathered the notes up and tucked them inside his waistband before leaning over her. Abby's natural instincts kicked in, and she lifted her arms to protect herself.

"What are you doing in my drawer? You're not my *mudder*," the boy yelled.

He didn't strike her, and she lowered her arms. He stood in front of the dresser, stuffing the clothes back inside with stiff, furious movements. He released a low sob, and that's when she realized he was crying. The notes had obviously meant more to him than he'd let on. Otherwise, he wouldn't have kept them. But he didn't want to admit it.

Because she wasn't his mother.

She stood and walked to him, moving nice and slow. In the past, her inclination whenever she faced physical conflict was to run from the room and find a safe place to hide until it blew over. But now, she forced herself to be brave. To put this motherless boy's needs before her own.

"Reuben, I didn't mean any harm." She spoke in a soothing tone. "I just found the notes when

I was putting your mended clothing away. I'm sorry. I didn't mean to pry."

He slammed the drawer closed, then brushed at his eyes. "You don't belong here. Why don't you leave?"

Ah, that hurt, like a knife to her heart.

"I can't," she said.

Finally, he faced her, his eyes red with resentment and tears. "Why not? Why do you have to stay here?"

"Because I have nowhere else to go." She said the words simply, making no apology.

His little jaw quivered, his face filled with misery. "Why can't you go back to Ohio?"

She looked away, not wanting to explain. "There's nothing there for me anymore."

He sniffled again. "But they're your *familye*. We're not."

"I know, but you've been *wundervoll* friends. Why did you keep the notes I put in your lunches?"

He hesitated. "Be…because I liked them. They made me feel *gut*."

He hiccupped and hid his face behind his hands, as if the admission was shameful to him.

"Then why did you say you never saw them?" She spoke gently, trying not to frighten or anger him. Determined to get at the crux of the problem.

"Because you're not my *mamm*, and I don't want her to think I don't love her anymore."

Finally. Finally, they were getting somewhere.

"Reuben, I don't want to take your *mudder's* place. I know how special she was to you. But I doubt she would ever think that you don't love her just because you were friends with me. And I wish I could bring her back to you. But I can't."

He leaned against the top of the dresser and buried his face against his arms. His shoulders trembled and he made little gasping sounds, telling her that he was crying again. Her heart went out to him. He'd lost so much, and she longed to ease his pain.

She stepped closer and rested a hand lightly against his back, fully expecting him to thrust her away. But he didn't. Not this time.

"Reuben, your *mudder* will always be a part of you, no matter what. You can take joy in that. You'll meet many people throughout your life, but no one can ever take her place. Not me, not anyone."

He lifted his head and blinked at her, a large tear rolling down his cheek. "Do you...do you mean that?"

"I do. I don't want you to forget your *mudder*. Even though she died, I certainly haven't forgotten mine. I just want to work and live here for the time being. I just want to be your friend."

"Friends?" he reiterated, wiping his nose on his sleeve.

She nodded. "*Ja*, I'd like that very much."

"Would I have to stop loving *Mamm* just because I decide to like you?" He peered at her with a bit of distrust.

She realized he must be struggling with guilt. That he believed it would be disloyal to his mother if he accepted her. Maybe Jakob was struggling with the same problem.

"Absolutely not. Liking me has nothing to do with loving your *mudder*. We're two separate individuals. And the amazing thing about love is that it's infinite."

"Infinite? What does that mean?" he asked.

"It means immeasurable. Boundless. You see, love can grow and expand within our hearts and never run out. Think about how our Heavenly *Vadder* loves all of His children. That's a lot of people to love, isn't it? But *Gott's* love never ends. It just keeps growing and encompasses everyone. And just like Him, we can love more than one person. But loving someone else doesn't mean that you have to stop loving your *mamm*. It doesn't change the relationship you had with her. Not ever. That's why love is so amazing and beautiful."

The boy gave a slight shudder, his forehead creased in thought. And then he threw himself against her, his tearstained face pressed against her abdomen as he hugged her tight.

"I'm sorry, Abby. I like you. I do. I want to be friends. But my *mamm*…" His desperate words were muffled against her apron.

She held him close, brushing a hand through his tousled hair. Her heart melted, a full, powerful sensation filling her chest. "There, it's all right now. We are *gut* friends. I like you, too."

In fact, she loved this boy, but didn't dare say so. Not right now, when their relationship was so fledgling. Perhaps in time.

He drew back and brushed at his face again. He gave her a wan smile. "I'm sorry for putting cracker crumbs in your bed."

She arched one eyebrow. "And filling my shoes with dirt?"

"*Ja*, I'm sorry for that, too."

She laughed, reaching out to playfully buffet his shoulder with the palm of her hand. He laughed, too.

"I know. I forgive you. But I'm glad we can laugh about it now," she said.

"It wasn't very nice of me. I can't believe you didn't tell *Daed* what I did."

"What good would it have done to get you into trouble with your *vadder*? I knew you were just feeling threatened and that you missed your *mudder* more than you could stand."

"*Ja*, I miss her every day. But I won't do anything like that to you ever again. I promise," he said.

"*Gut*. I'm so glad. I always knew you were a kindhearted boy."

"You did? But I've been so mean to you. How did you know?"

"Only a tenderhearted person could love his *mudder* the way you do. I'm sorry I made you worry."

He shrugged. "You're just looking for a home of your own. I'm sorry I wasn't more welcoming. You're our guest and I should have been kind."

She smiled to show him that all was forgiven. They looked at each other for a moment, and she breathed an inward sigh of relief, so happy to be rid of the animosity between them.

"*Ach*, I'd better get downstairs. Naomi is probably needing my help with the baking," Abby said.

She picked up her basket, giving him one last smile of reassurance. He grinned back, showing a tooth missing in front.

As she headed toward the door, she heard a

scuffling sound on the landing. She reached the threshold just as the door to Naomi's room was closing, which seemed odd. Abby thought the woman was downstairs in the kitchen, baking bread. Maybe Naomi had come upstairs for something.

Thinking nothing of it, Abby hurried on her way, feeling suddenly light of heart. She was so grateful that she and Reuben had finally become friends. That they had agreed upon a truce and he could finally accept her. If only Jakob could do the same, she'd be a happy woman indeed.

Jakob stood inside his mother's room and leaned against the closed door. Whew! That was a close call. Abby had almost caught him eavesdropping on the landing. He'd been downstairs when he heard Reuben yelling and had come up to see what the trouble was. When he'd arrived, he'd heard his son crying and then the boy's apology for being so mean to Abby. The boy had mentioned something about putting cracker crumbs between her sheets and dirt in her shoes. Jakob was mortified at the extent of his son's hostility. But why hadn't Abby told him about it? Why had she suffered in silence? She'd told Reuben that she didn't want to get him into trouble. But what about Abby? Jakob felt horrible that his son had done such things to her, yet her patience and kindness was inspiring.

Instead of criticizing the boy, she'd offered soft words of forgiveness and reassurance. In spite of her upbringing, she'd shown compassion when she could have been cruel. She could have let Reuben squirm for a while and think about his hostile actions. But Jakob had learned that Abby wasn't that way. She was quick to forgive, her bright blue eyes shining with empathy. Quick to offer solace for an aching heart. Her charity toward his *familye* impressed him. In fact, he'd never met anyone like her. Not even Susan had been so forgiving. And once again, Jakob was grateful for her gentle kindness toward his *familye*.

According to the book of I Corinthians, charity suffered long, was kind and envied not. It was not puffed up with pride, anger or vengeance. Because charity was the pure love of Christ, it took love to a higher level. A level that transcended earthly life and became eternal. It saw beyond the moment and rose to the level of the Savior. Yes, *charitable* described Abby perfectly.

Opening the door to his mother's room, Jakob peeked out to find that he was alone. Stepping onto the landing, he closed the door silently behind him, then hurried down the stairs. ~~Avoiding the kitchen and the women he~~ thought were working there, he crossed through the living room and walked outside onto the front porch.

Love is infinite.

Abby's words filtered through his mind. She'd told Reuben that loving someone else didn't mean he had to stop loving his *mamm*. In his heart of hearts, Jakob knew what Abby said was true. Yet, it still confused him. He had loved Susan so much that he thought he never could love someone else.

Correction. He still loved Susan with all his might, mind and strength. But now, he had to reevaluate his feelings. If he believed the scriptures and what Abby said, he should be able to keep loving Susan and still be able to love another with the same deep sincerity he'd felt for his wife. But how could that be? How could he give his heart to someone else when he was still so in love with Susan? Maybe he didn't have to stop loving his wife in order to love and find happiness with another woman. It was something to think about.

Crossing the lawn, he headed toward the backyard. As he rounded the corner of the house, he came up short. Abby was bent at the waist, digging in the garden. He would have slipped away to the barn, but she stood straight at that moment, saw him and waved. Her graceful fingers were caked with mud from pulling and cleaning radishes. With swift proficiency, she laid several of the red roots in one of the muck buckets she used for collecting vegetables. A basket sat nearby, filled with fresh lettuce and beet greens. As he drew near, a stray wisp of golden hair framed her flushed face and an endearing smear of dirt marred her delicate chin. Like the day when she'd planted the corn, she didn't seem to mind the dirt. In fact, she seemed perfectly at ease working with the earth.

Pulling several more radishes, she smiled up at him. "Since this is my first time growing a garden in Colorado, I'm not sure if it's doing well or not. There are so many vegetables I could grow in Ohio, but Naomi said they won't do well here."

"*Ne*, we have a much shorter growing season. We don't have as much water and we're at a higher elevation, so we get the frost sooner."

He glanced at the long rows filled with verdant green plants burgeoning in the fertile soil. Naomi had basically turned the garden completely over to Abby. Not a weed was in sight, and she'd been diligent about watering regularly, too. Again, he thought that she would make a perfect farmer's wife. Even her tomato plants were loaded with round, green fruit, attesting to the bountiful harvest they'd soon have…if they didn't get an early freeze. No one could fault her efforts.

"In spite of the growing difficulties we face here, your garden is doing very well," he said.

Her garden. It wasn't Susan's garden anymore. And somehow that no longer bothered him.

Using the back of her hand, she brushed the stray hair away from her face, then tossed a perplexed frown at the row of celery she'd tried to grow. Because the plants required lots of water, the stalks were dry and small. But Jakob knew that wasn't Abby's fault.

"Everything is doing well except for that." She gestured with disgust at the plants. "Naomi warned me not to try to grow celery here, but I wouldn't listen. I thought if I gave it lots of water and attention, I could make it work, but this soil doesn't seem to hold the water very well."

The Amish loved celery, using it in many of their food dishes. It was a sign of prosperity, and they grew extra for the wedding season. He knew it must be a disappointment to Abby that it wouldn't flourish here in Colorado.

She tilted her head, an accepting sigh escaping her full lips. "I guess I'll just have to get used to the difference. I miss the gardens I could grow in Ohio, but I've never seen anything more beautiful than the tall Rocky Mountains and the wide Arkansas River."

She gazed toward the East where the Sangre de Cristo Mountains stood like a great sentinel guarding the valley. With the lush green and purple mountains as a backdrop, she looked beautiful and lonely standing there. A plain woman with no makeup and frills, yet Jakob thought he'd never seen a more beautiful woman in all his life. A powerful urge swept over him to take her into his arms and hold her close against his heart.

"Don't worry. We can buy whatever celery you might need at the store in town," he said.

"I suppose so, but it's not quite the same as growing your own," she said.

He couldn't take his eyes off her. He stared at her sweet profile, suddenly yearning to make her happy, to see her smile and hear her laughter again.

"Maybe next year, we can plant some celery along Grape Creek. Wild asparagus grows well along the creek banks, so why not celery?" he asked.

That thought gave him pause. Next year, if she was still here.

She rested one hand at her waist and gazed at him in awe. When she spoke, her voice was filled with wonder and delight. "Do you really think so? It would be *wundervoll* if I could make celery grow here. I don't mind going out to the fields to tend it if it means we can grow our own."

A surge of admiration swept over him. Nothing seemed to intimidate Abby. So hardworking and energetic. So eager to try new things.

"All we can do is try," he said, a hard lump suddenly clogging his throat.

"*Ach*, I may not be here next year, but if I am, we'll give it a try," she said.

He hated to hear his own sad thoughts spoken aloud, but he couldn't fight the truth. If Martin Hostetler had his way, she'd marry him and be living at his farm next year. And Jakob didn't want that. No, not at all. Which brought him to what was really troubling him this afternoon.

"Abby, I overheard part of your conversation with Reuben a little while ago." He made the confession before he could change his mind. And once again, he thought how easy it was to confide in her.

Her eyebrows drew together in a doubtful frown. "You did?"

"*Ja*, I had come upstairs when I heard him

yelling, but then I didn't want to interfere. I realized it was a big moment for the two of you."

"*Ja*, it was," she said, smiling with satisfaction.

"I just wanted to say that I appreciate what you did for my son. I've spoken to him many times about his *mudder*, but nothing I've ever said has sunk in. You've been kind, and I'm grateful. Maybe he can finally start to heal now."

And maybe he could heal, too.

"You're *willkomm*. I just hope I really helped him see that he doesn't have to forget his *mudder*. She'll always be a part of each of you," she said, her voice very quiet.

"I know it hasn't been easy for you either, moving to a strange land, expecting to marry and all."

He paused, waiting for her to speak. Wishing she would say something to make this easier on him. But she didn't say a word. Just gazed at him with those dazzling blue eyes and an indulgent, noncommittal expression on her face.

"If…if I can have a little more time, I think perhaps I might be able to…" A yell cut him off before he could finish his thought.

"Jakob! Abby! *Kumme inwennich*."

They both turned and saw *Dawdi* Zeke wav-

ing urgently from the back porch, asking them
to come inside.

"What is it?" Jakob called, taking a step toward his grandfather.

"Bishop Yoder is here. He says it is urgent
that he speak with both of you."

The bishop was here? Not an odd occurrence
on any given day. Bishop Yoder frequently
called on the *familye* in the early evening for
no apparent reason. Jakob knew the man did
the same with other members of their congregation. It was the bishop's way of watching over
his flock, seeing to their needs and ensuring
they were living their faith. But what could be
so urgent that the bishop would show up here
in the middle of the workday?

As he and Abby walked toward the house,
Jakob wondered what could be so important
that Bishop Yoder had to speak with both him
and Abby right now. A bad feeling settled in
the pit of Jakob's stomach. Deep down, he knew
that the bishop's visit did not bode well for either him or Abby.

Chapter Thirteen

Dawdi Zeke held the door open for her as Abby stepped inside the kitchen. The fragrant aroma of fresh-baked bread enveloped her. Six loaves sat cooling on the table and would feed the *familye* for the week.

Setting her basket of vegetables on the counter beside the sink, she waggled her dirty fingers at Zeke. "I'll just wash up first, if that's all right."

"Of course. Come in when you're ready." The elderly man nodded and disappeared into the other room.

Picking up a bar of homemade soap scented with vanilla, she washed her hands. A heavy weight settled across her chest. What could Bishop Yoder want to see both her and Jakob about? Whatever it was, she didn't think it could be good. She found herself wishing that people would just forget about her and leave her alone. She was happy here at the Fishers' farm and longed for the time and freedom to thrive. But some innate sense warned her that the bishop was about to upset her life once more. She didn't know why or how, but she knew her life was about to make another drastic change.

She spent extra time cleaning the dirt out from under her short fingernails. As she lathered her skin, she was highly conscious of Jakob standing nearby, waiting for her to finish. She longed to confide her fears to him, but didn't dare. She had told him enough already and didn't want to get any closer to him.

"Are you all right?" he asked, his voice sounding subdued. Maybe he also sensed that something was about to change.

"*Ja.*"

But no, she wasn't. Not really. Ah, she was being silly. The bishop had probably come for a routine visit. He'd probably summoned her and Jakob simply because they were part of the same household and he wanted to visit with the entire *familye*. She was worrying about nothing.

Finally, she rinsed and Jakob handed her a towel to dry her hands, then accompanied her into the living room. He startled her when he rested his hand against her left shoulder blade for just a second, waiting for her to precede him into the room. His touch was gentle and warm, increasing her awareness of him. But it also brought her some small comfort. His presence made her feel safe somehow.

Bishop Yoder sat on the sofa, his straw hat in his hands. Naomi sat across from him in her rocking chair, nervously twisting her black apron strings around her fingers. *Dawdi* Zeke sat in his battered recliner. But where were the children? If this was a routine visit, Ruby and Reuben would be here, too. Since they were absent, that meant this was not routine at all.

"*Ach*, here they are," Naomi said. She patted her *kapp* and showed a nervous smile.

"*Hallo*, Jakob. *Vee gehts?*" The bishop stood and greeted him with a handshake.

"*Gut*, we are all well. *Danke,*" Jakob said.

"And you, Abby? *Vee gehts?*" The bishop took both of her hands in his, looking deeply into her eyes.

Abby saw a mixture of sympathy and concern in the man's gray eyes…a combination that once again put her on edge. What was going on?

She showed a half smile. "I am well, *danke*."

"*Gut. Gut.*"

With the niceties over, they all sat and the bishop took a deep inhale, as though resigning himself. Then, he reached into his hat and pulled out what appeared to be an envelope.

"I received a letter from Abby's brother this morning," he told them.

Abby's thoughts scattered. She sat up straighter, her pulse beating madly against her temples. Although she'd written to him several times, Simon had not replied once in all the weeks she'd been here.

"Wh…what did Simon have to say?" she asked, her voice wobbling. She clenched her hands together in her lap to keep them from trembling. She didn't understand why she should be upset by this meeting. Simon was far, far away and could no longer hurt her. Right?

Bishop Yoder cleared his throat, looking intense and uncomfortable. "He has demanded that you return to Ohio at once."

Naomi gasped. "What? But why?"

The bishop met Abby's gaze. "He claims that he didn't know where you had run off to, and as the patriarch of your *familye*, he feels responsible for your well-being. He is appalled that you are staying here in Jakob's home without benefit of marriage, and he demands your immediate return."

"But…but that's not true. Simon knew where I was going, otherwise how would he have known where to write to you?" she said, feeling outraged that her brother would lie about such a thing.

"He claims that a member of our district wrote to tell him that you were here and that you were unmarried," Bishop Yoder said.

"That might be true, but I've also written to Simon several times. Although he's never written back. He has known very well where I have been," she said.

The bishop studied her face, as though searching for the truth there. "He said that you had run away in the middle of the night. He is eager for your return."

Dawdi Zeke *harrumphed* at the implication. Naomi's eyes widened in outrage. Abby understood the allegation full well. With his letter, Simon was claiming that she'd betrayed him and her *familye* by leaving home in secrecy. That she had lied to the bishop and the Fisher *familye* when she'd told them that her brother knew where she was.

"*Ne*, it isn't true. He knew everything. I have never lied to him, nor to you. Not once," Abby said, the heat of outrage and embarrassment flowing over her entire body. How dare her brother discredit her like this to Bishop Yoder and the Fisher *familye*. It was offensive, cruel, shameful and...

Evil.

"May I see the letter?" Jakob asked humbly, holding out his hand.

The bishop passed the envelope to him. Everyone seemed to hold their breath as he opened and scanned the pages. His face remained passive, but Abby noticed that his shoulders had tensed. As he read, his jaw hardened like granite and his eyes narrowed. While other people might miss the signs, she knew him well enough to realize that he was upset by what he read, but endeavored to maintain his self-control. Finally, he tucked the papers back inside the envelope and returned it to the bishop.

"It states that, since Abby is not married, she must return to Ohio," Jakob said.

The bishop nodded. "*Ja*, that is correct."

"*Ach*, that alone tells me that he knew Abby's purpose in coming here. He knew that she planned to marry me."

Bishop Yoder looked at Abby. "I understand that Martin Hostetler has been courting you quite seriously."

Abby almost snorted. Not once had she gone out with Martin, and she found it almost comical that his few visits to the farm and their conversations at church could be called a serious courtship. Martin might be interested in her, but she wasn't interested in him. And that was that.

She shook her head. "I'm afraid that is rather one-sided, but I still want to remain here. Please don't make me go back. Please."

Okay, she'd resorted to begging again. But at this point, she'd do anything not to return to the harsh life awaiting her in her brother's home.

"I'm sorry, Abby," Bishop Yoder said. "But your *bruder* is the head of your *familye* now that your *vadder* is gone. If you were married, things would be different. But as a single woman, you must respect Simon as the patriarch of your home. You must obey him and return to Ohio."

No, no! She didn't want to obey her brother. She longed to make choices for herself, to escape the domination of any man. Surely *Gott* did not condone the abuse she had suffered. Surely it was wrong. But even as she thought these things, she knew it was no use. She did not believe that *Gott* approved of her brother's actions, but neither did He approve of her disobedience. He would want her to bear her burdens humbly and meekly, with long-suffering and no murmuring.

Blinking back tears of disappointment, she bowed her head in submission. In her heart, she was willing to suffer anything as long as she could retain her relationship with *Gott*. If she had to return to Ohio, then the Lord must have something else in mind for her. She had to believe that. She must! Because nothing was more important to her than her faith. She must wait upon *Gott's* will.

"What if Abby were to marry right now?" Jakob asked.

Abby lifted her head and stared at the man, wondering what he was saying. If he suggested she marry Martin Hostetler just to keep from going back to Ohio, she couldn't do it. Not only was she not interested, but Martin also deserved to wed a woman who truly loved him.

Bishop Yoder shrugged. "Then her first duty would be to remain with her husband. Do you have a proposal in mind?"

A long silence followed, weighed down by a morose confusion. Abby held her breath, wondering what Jakob would say. She didn't know what to think at this point. Nor did she dare hold out any hope. She loved Jakob. She always had, since they were children. She loved him, but he didn't love her. It was that simple. He had made it clear on numerous occasions that he still longed for his dead wife. That his heart was too full of memories of Susan to make any room for another. Loving Abby was an impossibility. Nothing could save her now. Not even Jakob. She had no choice but to return to Simon in Ohio.

* * *

"I will marry Abby." Jakob said the words before he could change his mind.

Her low cry of surprise sounded like a shout in the quiet room. He knew his proposal startled her, but he wouldn't take it back. Not when he knew the abuse she would be subjected to if she returned to her brother. His conscience wouldn't allow him to do that. Not when he knew that he could prevent it. Even if they had a marriage in name only, it would be better than sending her away. He couldn't do that. He couldn't.

"Oh, Jakob! How *wundervoll*." Naomi clasped her hands together in an exclamation of joy.

Dawdi Zeke grinned and nodded with approval, his spectacles sliding down his nose. "*Ja*, it's the right thing to do. I wholeheartedly approve."

Even Bishop Yoder smiled. And now that Abby had made friends with Reuben, Jakob believed his two children would be delighted, too. Marrying Abby would fix everyone's problems. It would bring stability to his home. She'd already become a member of the *familye*. They should make it permanent and official. She could stay here and she'd be safe. It was the right thing to do. Wasn't it?

"May I speak with Jakob in private, please?"

Jakob turned to see Abby sitting primly with her hands folded in her lap. Her back was stiff, her neck straight, a calm yet resolute expression on her face.

She stood and turned toward the door without waiting for anyone to speak. In automatic response, Jakob followed her outside, wondering what she was thinking. What if she refused his proposal? Surely she wouldn't do such a thing. Not when she knew the alternative.

Outside, he expected her to sit on the front porch, but she kept going. Down the stairs, across the green lawn and toward the fence line bordering the cornfield...where no one could listen through open windows and eavesdrop on their conversation.

Beneath the spread of a hackberry tree, she finally stopped and turned to face him. Lifting her chin two inches higher, she locked her gaze with his.

"Do you love me, Jakob?" Her words were spoken so quietly that he almost didn't hear.

He paused, his mind churning. He loved Susan. He always would. But did he love Abby, too? Did he?

"This is what I wanted to talk with you about earlier, when we were interrupted by the bishop's visit," he said. "I... I have come to care for you a great deal, Abby. In fact, I want you to stay here, with my *familye*. I don't want you to leave."

She shifted her weight and folded her arms. "I know you care for me and that we are *gut* friends. But since I came here, my feelings have changed. I don't want to be second-best. I want more from the man I marry. Do you love me?"

"Abby, I… I need more time. I've caught glimpses of how it could be between us, but I still don't know," he said, wishing he could make sense of his feelings. He knew he didn't want her to leave. That he was desperate for her to stay. Yes, he'd overheard Abby telling Reuben that he could love his mother and still be friends with her. Jakob's common sense told him that he could do the same with Susan. He could love both her and Abby. But a deep part of Jakob's heart wouldn't let him make that leap.

"*Ne*, Jakob. If you loved me, you would know in here." She placed the palm of her hand against his chest.

Her touch was warm and gentle, setting his heart to racing. He longed to pull her into his arms and offer her some reassurance. He was physically attracted to her. He enjoyed being with her. But did he love her?

"I want to marry you, Abby. To make a *fami-*

lye with you. I don't want you to go. In time, I believe I would—"

She shook her head, interrupting him. "*Ne*, Jakob. We are out of time. As tempting as your offer is, I will not accept a pity marriage. Not from you and not from any other man."

He snorted. "Believe me, my offer is certainly not out of pity, Abby. Any man would be blessed to marry you. I'm very aware of how beautiful and superb you are. Against great adversity, you have followed the rules of the *Ordnung* all the days of your life. Your faith inspires me to be a better man, to do more *gut*. You're everything I could ever want in a wife. It's me who should throw myself on your mercy. I'm the one who is so deficient."

And he sensed that she could help him find the answers. Today, he'd felt as though he were on the cusp of discovering something transcendent about himself, but Bishop Yoder had interrupted them. Now it was as if he couldn't wave away the fog so he could see what was hidden so clearly in his own mind. It had been there, then it was gone and he couldn't find it again. He didn't even know what it was he felt for Abby. She was unique. His feelings for her were so different from what he'd felt for Susan. He only knew he was desperate for her to remain here with him.

"You are very kind, and I thank you for your offer," she said, showing a sad little smile.

"But…?"

"But a marriage without love would not be *gut* for either of us. When I finally wed, it will be to a man who adores me. A kind, generous man who puts me above all others, except *Gott*."

"I do, Abby. I mean, I will do all of that."

She scoffed. "You care for me like you do all the members of our congregation. Like you would a neighbor or dear friend. But not as a wife. Not as a cherished partner to toil and live each day of our lives together. If we wed, you would eventually come to resent me. You would feel trapped. And I would feel like a castoff. Like a second-class burden no one else wanted. I couldn't live like that, Jakob. I'm not asking you to give up your love for Susan, but I am asking you to love me just as much as you loved her. Can you do that?"

Here it was. He blinked in confusion, wondering if he could. It was a novel idea to him. How could he love both women equally at the same time?

"I… I don't know. You are both so different, yet you are both so *wundervoll*. It's like comparing wheat to corn. I want both of them, but I married Susan first and still feel loyal to her."

She laughed and it was so good to see her smile again, but not like this.

"Only a farmer would make such an analogy," she said.

"*Ach*, I am a plain man and I make no apologies for it. It is who I am, who I will always be. You would need to accept me for who I am, just as I must accept you."

"You don't need to apologize, Jakob," she said. "You are a *gut* man of faith, and any woman would be honored to accept your marriage proposal. One day, I hope you find what you are seeking."

He couldn't believe what she was saying. "Are you turning me down, then?"

"Yes, Jakob, I am."

He stared at her, stunned to the tips of his scuffed work boots. Not because she was refusing him, but because she fully knew what would happen if she did. "You would rather return to Simon and his abuse than to marry me and remain here in Colorado with my *familye*?"

"*Ne*, of course not. I would love nothing more than to stay here. I love Naomi and Zeke. And I adore Ruby and Reuben. But I would rather suffer Simon's abuse than live here and love you, yet know in my heart that you don't love me in return."

She loved him? That was a startling realization. It touched a deep part of his heart. Knowing that she loved him, he wanted even more to protect her. To not hurt her ever.

What he felt for Abby was powerful. They were close friends. Weren't they? But was friends enough for marriage? Were his feelings as strong as what he had felt for Susan?

His love for Susan was still in the present, wasn't it? He still loved her. And yet, his feelings had changed somehow. She was the mother of his children. He had cherished her. But now, Abby was here in his life and Susan was gone.

A blaze of frustration scorched his senses. He wanted to give Abby what she asked for. To love and cherish her as a man should love and cherish his wife. But he was so afraid. What if he couldn't do it? What if it wasn't in him to love more than one woman that way? And if he did, how could he stand the pain if he lost her the way he'd lost Susan?

"Let's not make any decisions right now," he said. "I will ask Bishop Yoder to delay your return to Ohio a little longer."

She was silent for a moment, considering his words with a perplexed frown. The corners of her eyes crinkled as she squinted against the bright spray of summer sunlight. In spite of working outside with him each day, not a single freckle marred her smooth complexion. He remained perfectly still, holding his breath. Giving her time to consider his suggestion. The wind rustled her skirts, whipping them against her slender ankles.

"I don't think more time will make any difference for either of us," she said. "We both know what we want, and neither of us can have it. She's not coming back, Jakob. You know that, don't you?"

Abby's words struck him like a fist to the face. Yes, he knew it, but maybe he was just now starting to accept it.

"I will return to Ohio where I belong," she said with finality.

"*Ne*, I will ask the bishop for more time before he replies to your *bruder*. *Gehne mir!* We'll go now and tell Bishop Yoder of our request."

To keep her from refusing, he reached out and took her hand in his, pulling her gently with him toward the house. She didn't fight him, and he was relieved. Her agreement meant everything. This was the best solution. It would buy them more time together. And tomorrow, he would take her for a buggy ride in the afternoon, just the two of them. He would court her. Hold her hand. Maybe even kiss her. They would have time to get to know each other on a romantic level.

Time to convince her to marry him.

Inside the house, he quickly made his request to the bishop. *Dawdi* Zeke remained stoic, his bushy eyebrows pulled together in a frown. Naomi looked worried, too, but Bishop Yoder nodded his assent.

"I would like nothing more than to have Abby remain here within our community," the bishop said. "I will delay in responding to your *bruder* for a brief amount of time. But then, Abby will need to go back."

Abby stood silently holding her hands together in front of her. She didn't speak, nod or move a muscle. Her eyes were wide, her face ashen. And that's when Jakob felt the futility of his request. Time would make no difference. It wouldn't change anything between them. Nothing would, and he realized he'd have to face up to it.

Chapter Fourteen

"Do you want me to cut some more wood?"

Jakob paused as he sanded a piece of cedarwood and looked at *Dawdi* Zeke. Standing inside the workshop, the elderly man indicated a neatly stacked pile of wood scraps on the other side of the workbench.

"*Ne*, I think we have enough cut already."

Jakob glanced at the row of birdhouses lining the tall shelf. He and *Dawdi* Zeke supplied the hardware store in town with an assortment of birdhouses, feeders and wishing wells, selling them on consignment. Tourists loved the gaily painted fixtures, which were another source of income for them. And they were easy to produce, made from scraps of wood left over from larger projects. If Abby helped *Dawdi* Zeke paint, they might be able to sell them in some of the neighboring towns, too.

Abby. He'd thought of little else since Bishop Yoder had left over two hours earlier. Beneath the warm glow of kerosene light, he rubbed his fingers along the grain of the wood, feeling for any rough edges. He needed time to think. To come up with a plan. Some way to protect Abby from her brother. But nothing came to mind.

"What are you gonna do about Abby?" *Dawdi* Zeke asked.

Hmm. Jakob had to give his grandfather credit. The elderly man hadn't said a word about her since the bishop had left. But now, *Dawdi* seemed to be growing restless.

After wiping the surface of the wood with a tack cloth, Jakob shook it out. A small cloud of dust made him cough. "I'm not sure yet. I hope she will stay here and decide to wed me."

Dawdi Zeke picked up a brush and dabbed red paint on the top of a miniature roof. "*Ach*, no doubt she's feeling like she'll always be in second place if she marries you."

Jakob didn't ask why. He knew *Dawdi* was right, but he didn't want Abby to feel that way. She deserved better than that. She was so wonderful that he wanted her to feel happy and secure in their marriage, not as if she were a last resort.

"She's made it clear that she won't marry a man who doesn't love her," Jakob said.

And that was the crux of the problem. Jakob couldn't love her. If she died the way Susan had done, he couldn't face that loss again. Neither could his children. So where did that leave them? Nowhere!

Dawdi Zeke nodded. "I can understand her feelings. My second wife felt the same way."

Jakob jerked his head up, his mouth dropping open in surprise. He'd known since he was a toddler that *Dawdi* Zeke had been married twice, but he had no idea his grandmother felt second-best. "You mean my *grossmammi* felt like that?"

"*Ja*, for several years, until I convinced her differently. My first wife was Maddie. You never knew her, she died long before you were born. She had auburn hair and the prettiest hazel eyes you ever saw. She died of pneumonia when she was only nineteen years old. She was four months along with our first child."

Jakob's heart wrenched with sadness. Although he'd known about Maddie, he hadn't realized she was expecting a baby. His grandfather's story reminded him that he wasn't the only one who had lost a beloved wife and unborn child. In spite of his sorrows, Jakob had so much to be grateful for. He just had to look for the good and count his many blessings.

"*Ach*, I'm sorry, *Dawdi*."

"There's no need to be sorry. Maddie is with the *gut* Lord now. She's happy and content, and I hope I'm worthy to see her again one day," *Dawdi* Zeke said.

The elderly man was silent for a few moments and a faraway look filled his eyes, as though he were remembering back to his youth.

"There was a time when I didn't think I could stand the loss," he said. "I was barely twenty years old at the time. It took a long thirteen years before I could move on. I was thirty-three before I wed again. Helen, your *grossmammi*, was the *mudder* of my seven *kinder*. We were married sixty years. She was so talented, sweet, kind and sensible. A hard worker who loved *Gott* more than anything else. Her faith meant everything to her. I came to depend on her and loved her like I've never loved anyone in my life, and I miss her every moment of every day."

"But if you loved Maddie so much, how did you let your heart come to love my *grossmammi*, too?" Jakob asked.

Dawdi Zeke shrugged. "Over the years, I missed my Maddie. If she had lived, I have no doubt we would have been married all our lives. But then I wouldn't have known Helen and the joy we shared. Now, I'm a very old man, but my heart still feels young when I think about the two women who shared my heart. Even though they were so different, I loved them equally. ~~I could never choose between them~~. And now that I face meeting *Gott* soon, I can't say that I would change a thing. He knew what I needed to make me grow in faith. I faced a lot of pain losing Maddie, but He's never deserted me. Not once."

Jakob thought about his grandfather's words for several moments. "But when you loved Helen, didn't you feel disloyal to Maddie?"

Dawdi Zeke tilted his head, his bushy gray eyebrows drawn together in confusion. "What for?"

Jakob thought it was obvious, but explained anyway. "For loving another woman."

"Ne!" *Dawdi* Zeke waved a hand. "I loved both women at different times. There was nothing wrong in that. I loved them, just as *Gott* loves them. I couldn't choose between the two. My Maddie wouldn't have wanted me to go on living my life alone and unhappy. It's *Gott's* plan that we wed and raise a *familye*. That's what makes up eternity. Our *familye*. And if I hadn't loved and married Helen, I never would have had *kinder*. I wouldn't have you."

Jakob had never thought about that. What if he was supposed to marry Abby and have more children with her? If he let her go, he might be letting her down. He might be letting *Gott* down, too.

Dawdi Zeke gave him a gentle wink. "I understand what you're going through, *mein sohn.* I truly do. You want to love and be loyal to Susan, but that won't help Abby. She needs you now. Don't wait thirteen years to learn the lesson I learned. Be at peace. Don't forget your faith. *Gott* has a plan for you. When we think all is lost, sometimes He can surprise us. Let Susan go now. Hold on to your faith and Abby."

As his grandfather stepped away, Jakob found it suddenly so easy to feel the older man's confidence in *Gott.* To feel so light of heart. He'd loved Susan, but now she was gone. She was at peace, but he hadn't been. Not for months.

Jakob thought about after the Sermon on the Mount, when the Savior left in a boat. He was awakened by his disciples to find a great storm waging around them. That was how Jakob had felt since Susan died. His heart and mind had been in constant turmoil, battered by doubts and fear. But Jesus was the Prince of Peace. He had calmed the angry storm and taught a powerful lesson. That when we have faith and rely on Him, we also can have peace no matter what storms life throws our way.

Christ's example spoke with strength to

Jakob now. And suddenly, it was so easy to hand his burdens over to the Lord. To let go of his anguish and doubts. To rely on Christ, his Savior and friend. He would go forward in faith, confident and firm in his trust that *Gott* would show him the way. No longer would he be afraid.

He paused, that thought filling his mind. He wasn't afraid anymore. In fact, the possibilities suddenly seemed endless. He'd been holding back his feelings for Abby out of guilt and fear of losing her. But that had to change.

Glancing at the open door, he saw the dark sky filled with shining stars. Abby was probably asleep by now. Too late to seek her out and talk to her. And he could hardly wait for tomorrow.

That night, Abby read a bedtime story to Reuben and Ruby. She almost cried when both children cuddled up with her so they could see the pictures of the book. The fragrant smell of Naomi's vanilla soap wafted from their clean skin. Reuben slipped his hand over her arm and laughed at her attempts to lower her voice the way Jakob did. It seemed as though there had never been even a smidgen of animosity between them. When she finished the tale, Reuben climbed over to his bed. Abby tucked both children beneath their covers and kissed them each on the forehead.

"Have you been to your room yet this evening?" Reuben asked expectantly.

Abby gave him a quizzical look, wondering why he would ask such a thing. Hopefully he hadn't filled her clothes with thistles, or put soap in her hairbrush. They were beyond such childish pranks now, weren't they?

"*Ne*, why do you ask?"

He looked away, his cheeks flushing red. "No reason. I was just wondering."

Ruby stifled a wide yawn, her eyes drooping as she spoke in a sleepy, contented voice. "You'll never leave us will you, Abby?"

Abby froze, her heart squeezing hard. She didn't know what to say. The children weren't yet aware that Simon had summoned her home. They didn't know she would be leaving soon.

"*Ach*, *Mamm* left us. Everyone leaves eventually," Reuben said, his voice a bit begrudging.

"But your *mudder* didn't want to go," Abby said quietly. "Her body just gave out. She would have stayed with you forever if she could."

"How do you know?" Ruby asked.

Abby tickled the girl's ribs, making her giggle. "Because that's what *mudders* do. I feel the same way about you and Reuben. I'd stay with you forever if I could."

"*Daed* says *Mamm* and our baby *bruder* are with *Gott* now," Ruby said.

Abby nodded. "*Ja*, that's right."

Reuben peered at her, his wide, dark eyes seeming to look deep into her heart. "But you won't leave us. Not for a long time until you're very old. Will you?"

Abby took an inhale to steady her nerves. She didn't want to make promises she couldn't keep, but this conversation was breaking her heart. "I can't promise that, *liebchen*. None of us can promise to stay. But you know I'll always love both of you, don't you? I can promise that."

"*Ja*, and I love you, too," Ruby said, yawning again. "Tomorrow, *Grossmammi* said we're going to take the kittens out to the barn so we can get them used to their new home. Do you really think they'll be okay out there?"

Relieved to change the topic, Abby nodded. "I do."

"But what will they eat? They don't know how to catch mice yet. They'll be lonely out there in that big old drafty barn."

"They'll learn soon enough to catch mice, and they can curl up in the warm straw. Hunting will come naturally to them. And you can keep an eye on them to ensure they're not going hungry. If they are, you can give them some scraps from the kitchen to eat."

The babies had gotten so big since Abby had found them in the barn weeks earlier. They had grown fast, but Abby wouldn't be here to watch either the cats or the children grow into adulthood.

Tomorrow. Tomorrow she must leave. No matter how long the bishop delayed corresponding with her brother, she couldn't stay here any longer. She appreciated Jakob's efforts on her behalf, but she'd spent enough time with him that, if he didn't love her now, he never would. Staying longer would only exacerbate the situation. It would be pure torture, building up all of their hopes only to have them dashed. And in the end, she would have to return to Ohio anyway. It would be better to leave now than to spend more time with Jakob, knowing he could never love her. Her heart couldn't take that. Not anymore.

"Rest now," she said. "*Gott* will take care of you no matter what happens in your life. You just need to have faith and all will be well."

She blew out the kerosene lamp and left the door slightly ajar. Ruby rubbed her eyes again and Reuben rolled over. Abby peered at them through the dark, listening to their soft even breathing for several moments.

As she crossed the landing to her own room, she had to blink back tears. Never before had her faith been put to such a test, and she wondered what *Gott* had in store for her. She didn't want to leave, but knew if she refused, she could be censured by the church. She might even be shunned, which meant that Jakob and his *familye* couldn't speak or eat with her, nor take anything from her hand. She didn't want to put Bishop Yoder or the Fishers in that uncomfortable position. What would it accomplish, except to create more heartache for them all?

Pulling back the covers to her bed, she fluffed the pillow. A white scrap of paper fell to the floor. Picking it up, she read the words scrawled in childish handwriting: *You smell like apple blossoms.*

Folding the note, she closed her eyes and held the paper close against her heart. Tears squeezed from between her eyelashes. Now she understood why Reuben had asked if she'd been to her room this evening. She had absolutely no doubt that he had written this message and was wondering if she'd seen it yet.

She hadn't realized that she smelled like apple blossoms. It must be the homemade lotion Naomi had given to her. But the fact that Reuben had noticed and thought to comment on it touched her heart like nothing else could.

Once she was gone, who would write uplifting notes to put in Reuben's lunch pail? And who would comfort Ruby if one of the kittens went missing or got hurt? Naomi, *Dawdi* Zeke and Jakob would do all they could for both children, but Abby could hardly stand the thought of leaving them. Not now. Not when she loved them so much. Not when she still loved Jakob. Finally, for the first time in her life, she felt wanted and needed. Like this was her home. But it couldn't be helped. Nothing was going to change Jakob's heart. She had to leave.

The following morning, Abby was up early. As quietly as possible, she packed her battered suitcase. Its contents included the note Reuben had hidden beneath her pillow, a picture Ruby had drawn of the baby kittens scampering across the yard and the wild iris Jakob had picked for her in the cornfield. None of them would ever know how much she treasured these simple things or how much their gestures of kindness meant to her.

Stowing her suitcase under the bed where no one would see it, she went downstairs to do her chores. It was still dark outside as she crossed the yard to the barn, the crisp air filling her lungs. She found her wire basket for collecting eggs sitting on a bench just inside, filled with a bunch of silver lupines.

Her stomach did a myriad of flip-flops. Jakob must have picked the flowers for her, but it didn't mean he loved her. Still, his gesture touched her heart.

Lifting the bouquet, she pressed it to her nose and inhaled deeply of the sweet fragrance. She would add several of the violet flowers to her cherished possessions.

A flash of white caught her eye. Plucking it from the basket, she discovered a note addressed to her. As she opened it, her heart thudded and her hands shook like aspens in the wind.

Abby,
I'm sorry I missed you this morning. I left early so that I can finish my chores in time to take you for a buggy ride this afternoon. Mamm *will take the* kinder *with her to the quilting frolic, so you won't need to watch them. Please plan your workday so you can be ready to leave with me around noon.*
Jakob.

Abby's pulse tripped into double time. No one had ever left her a message like this before. No one had ever gone out of the way to plan a buggy ride with her. Martin Hostetler didn't count because she'd told him "no" several times. It was so tempting to stay and spend an enjoyable afternoon with Jakob, but his note was what convinced her it was time to go. She detected no affection in his words. No words of endearment. Nothing to indicate he was excited to spend the afternoon with her. He'd even signed the note simply with just his name. No emotion. No love.

She must not be sucked into false hope. Over the past few months, she'd spent plenty of time alone with Jakob, and he still didn't love her. Nothing would change with a bunch of flowers and a buggy ride, but she was grateful that he had at least made the effort. She didn't blame him. In fact, she admired him for his honesty and his loyalty to Susan. She just wished he could find room in his heart to love her, too.

Today, she would leave. *Dawdi* Zeke would spend most of his time inside the workshop. Naomi would take the children with her. Jakob was already out in the fields watering and weeding the crops. He wouldn't be back for hours. By the time the *familye* returned home, she'd be gone. It was a nine-mile walk to the bus depot in town, but she could make it. She'd leave a letter of explanation and go. It would be easier this way. No tearful goodbyes. No guilt or recriminations. They'd just quietly get on with their lives.

Tucking Jakob's note into the heel of her shoe, she hurried with her work. Thirty minutes later, she was back in the kitchen and greeted Naomi and the children with a cheerful smile and a kiss.

"*Danke* for your sweet note. It made me feel so happy," she told Reuben.

He smiled, looking suddenly shy as he took his seat.

The tantalizing aroma of sausage and cornmeal filled the air. As she spooned scrapple into their bowls, they didn't seem to notice anything different. It was just another ordinary day. And yet, Abby felt like crying.

"Did Jakob tell you that the *kinder* will be going with me to the quilting frolic this morning?" Naomi asked in a pleasant tone.

"*Ja*, he left me a note." Abby turned away so no one would see the tears in her eyes. She didn't want the woman to know that she wouldn't be here when Jakob returned. That she'd probably never see any of them again.

"I wish you could join us, but there will be plenty of time for you to attend other frolics another time," Naomi continued, seeming almost buoyant at the thought.

Abby didn't respond. No doubt the woman was eager for her eldest son to marry again. And why not? The Amish were taught to cherish their children. They valued *familye* second only to their obedience to *Gott*.

As she set a plate of warm biscuits on the table, the kittens mewed at Abby's feet. They wanted their breakfast, too. Looking up, she locked her gaze with *Dawdi* Zeke's. He hadn't picked up his spoon to eat and was watching her quietly, his gray eyes narrowed with shrewd intelligence. Did he know what she planned? Oh, she hoped not. Running away seemed dishonest somehow. She loved the elderly man and hated to do anything to lose his respect.

Turning away, Abby quickly filled a saucer with cream and tiny pieces of sausage. If this was the last time she would get to feed the kittens, she wanted to make it a good meal for them. She set the dish on the floor beside the stove and petted the two babies as they ate ravenously, their long tails high in the air.

Within an hour, Abby had washed the dishes and swept the floor, and was standing on the front porch, waving goodbye to Naomi and the children. Tears clouded her vision as she blew them a kiss. As predicted, Zeke had disappeared into the workshop. Now was her chance.

Hurrying inside, she ran upstairs to retrieve

her suitcase and the letter she'd written late last night addressed to the entire *familye*. In the kitchen, she placed the envelope in the middle of the table, where it was sure to be seen. After picking up the basket of food she had prepared for her journey, she opened the front door cautiously. She peered out, making certain *Dawdi* Zeke wasn't around. When she didn't see him, she scurried toward the main road, eager to put some distance between herself and the farm.

From past experience, she figured it would take three hours to walk the nine miles, which would put her in town around noon. That was roughly the time when Jakob would be ready to collect her for their buggy ride. If her memory was correct, a bus would be departing at one thirty. She'd be tired, but she could rest once she'd bought a ticket and was safely on her way to Ohio. But as she walked along the dusty road, she couldn't help feeling that all was lost.

Chapter Fifteen

"What do you mean Abby is gone?"

Jakob stood outside the barn and stared at his *familye* in disbelief. He'd returned home early from the fields, dusty and smelling of sweat. He didn't want Abby to see him like this and was eager to go to the *dawdy haus* so he could clean up before their buggy ride. In fact, he'd thought about nothing else all day long. Talking to her. Being with her.

"She's gone," *Dawdi* Zeke said again. "She left a letter for us on the table in the kitchen. She's walked into town, planning to board a bus back to Ohio today at one thirty."

One thirty? Jakob glanced at the azure sky. He didn't own a watch, but he knew from the position of the sun that it must be almost noon.

"Go after her, *Daed*. You have to bring her

back." Ruby stood beside Naomi, rubbing her tear-drenched eyes.

Reuben sniffled as he held *Dawdi* Zeke's hand. "*Ja, Daed*, go and get her. Hurry, before she's gone forever."

"*Ach*, Jakob. Don't let her leave," Naomi said.

A cold, sick feeling settled over Jakob. Abby was gone. She'd left without saying goodbye.

"But why? I thought we had more time. I left her a note this morning. Why would she leave without telling me?"

Dawdi Zeke shook his head. "You know why she left. Do I have to explain it again?"

No, Jakob knew. He'd always known. But he'd been in denial. He thought he could stave off the inevitable, but Abby was smarter than him. She knew they couldn't go on the way they had been. Their relationship had to move to the next level, or die.

And that's when the truth washed over him with the force of a tidal wave. He loved Abby. He always had, but he'd been so fearful. Afraid of loving and losing her the way he'd lost Susan. But now, he knew that he wanted to be with Abby. To hold her close and have more children with her. To plan for the future and grow old with her.

To marry and love her all the rest of his days.

Yes, he loved her. He could admit it now.

When he'd written the note to Abby and planned the buggy ride, he'd wanted to be near her but hadn't understood how he felt. Now, an overwhelming love enveloped him and he didn't push it away or try to ignore his feelings. He loved her; he was certain of it.

The revelation was like a thunderous epiphany. It came on so strongly that he couldn't deny it any longer. Something he'd always known deep inside, but just couldn't bring himself to admit. But it was there now. It had taken root within him and was growing fast. The fledgling, thrilling love that made him hopeful, expectant and anxious to be with her.

And now, he may have lost her for good.

He glanced at the buggy Naomi and the children had used to go to the quilting frolic. It was still hitched to Tommy. Reaching for the tugs on the harness, he spoke over his shoulder.

"Does anyone know when she left? Do I have time to ride into town before she's gone?"

He spoke in a rush over his shoulder, removing the harness hitched to the horse.

Dawdi Zeke helped him, pulling on the girth belt. "I suspect she left right after Naomi and the *kinder* went to the quilting frolic, but she would have been on foot. You've got to go after her, Jakob. Tell her the truth."

Jakob paused. Turned. "The truth?"

"*Ja*. That you *lieb* her. It's time you finally admitted it."

Yes, it was time. A flash of panic rushed over him. Not because he loved her. Oh, no. He felt the panic of dread, that he was about to lose something more precious than gold. He had to hurry, to get to town before the bus left. He couldn't let Abby go. Not now. Now when he'd finally realized how he really felt about her.

He turned toward the barn, intending to retrieve the only saddle they owned. There was no need. Reuben had gone after it for him, grunting as he half carried, half dragged the heavy leather toward the horse.

"*Danke, sohn.*" Jakob lifted the dusty apparatus easily and swung it and a horse blanket up onto Tommy's back. Although the Amish were good horsemen, they rarely rode horses. Not for recreational purposes, anyway. But this was an emergency.

The horse sidestepped, not used to being ridden. Jakob persisted, figuring he could move much swifter if he rode astride instead of driving the buggy. But that meant that Abby and her luggage would have to ride behind him on the way home. Right now, it couldn't be helped.

He didn't care about anything except reaching her before it was too late.

The bus was delayed. Some kind of engine failure.

Sitting on a hard chair inside the terminal, Abby glanced at the clock on the wall. Almost two o'clock. Jakob, Naomi and the *kinder* would have returned home by now. They would have found her note on the kitchen table. They'd be upset, wondering and wishing and crying. But it was best to get it over with and move on.

Someone coughed and she glanced over to where two *Englisch* women sat nearby, their heads bent close together as they discussed this delay. Another woman comforted her crying toddler while her husband checked his wristwatch, then shook his head with annoyance. Other passengers sat around, too, waiting inside the air-conditioned terminal instead of outside in the baking sunshine. Occasionally one of them looked at her, their curious expressions telling her they thought her plain appearance was rather odd. They all seemed as anxious as Abby to get on the bus and leave town.

Her battered suitcase and small basket sat beside her on the floor. She looked at the clock again, wishing Harry, the conductor with the blue name badge pinned to his shirtfront, would give them another update. If they couldn't get the bus working, she couldn't go back to the Fisher farm. She hated the thought of spending the night here and worried about what she would do.

Turning toward the door, she adjusted her black traveling bonnet and blinked. Jakob stood in the doorway, looking out of breath as he stared directly at her. Through the wide windows, she saw Tommy standing with his head down, blowing hard, his reins tied to the bike stand out front.

"Oh, *ne*."

She buried her face in her hands, her cheeks burning as hot as kerosene. If only the bus hadn't broken down, she'd be long gone now. What could she do? She didn't want to face him. It was too humiliating. Too sad. Too...

Someone touched her hand. She looked up into Jakob's eyes. In a glance, she took in his dusty clothes, his slightly damp hair and sparkling dark eyes. For a moment, she thought she saw relief pass over his face, but she must have imagined it.

"Hallo," he said, but he didn't smile.

"Wh...what are you doing here?" She couldn't move. Couldn't breathe.

"I came to bring you home where you belong."

His words confused her. Why would he come

after her if he didn't want her? He could just let her go, and no one would ever blame him for it.

"Folks," Harry called to get their attention. "I'm real sorry for the delay. We had an oil leak, but a new bus has just arrived. If you'll give us a few more minutes to fuel up, we'll be ready to leave soon. You can line up out front and we'll take your luggage now."

The passengers breathed a collective sigh of relief and started gathering up their things. A few more minutes and Abby would be on the bus, leaving behind her hopes and dreams of a happy life.

"I... I don't understand." No doubt he was feeling guilty, so he'd come after her. She didn't want to make it worse.

"I came for you. It's that simple." He sat beside her.

Feeling embarrassed, she stood and he did, too, following her every move.

"Jakob, you don't need to worry about me. I'll be fine, really. We aren't getting married, and that's that. There's no need to feel guilty about this."

"The only thing I feel guilty about is hurting you. But I didn't come here because of that. I came because I love you."

What? She shook her head, thinking she'd heard him wrong.

He held out his hands in a pleading gesture. "Just hear me out, Abby. Please."

She glanced toward the door, realizing she had only minutes before they would be boarding the bus. But she couldn't turn her back on him. Not now, not ever.

"When I learned you were gone, I couldn't stand to lose you. Last night, *Dawdi* Zeke helped me understand what I've been feeling. I've waited all day to tell you. That's why I planned a special buggy ride, so we could be alone. But then I got home and found out you had left."

"*Dawdi* Zeke?" She felt beyond confused. She hoped Zeke hadn't talked Jakob into marrying her.

Jakob quickly told her about Zeke's two wives. It was a touching story, but Abby didn't see how it could change anything between them.

"It wasn't until I spoke with him that I realized the truth. I love you, Abby. I always have. I just couldn't see it. My heart was too crowded by fear."

Oh, how she wanted to believe him, but she couldn't. Not without real proof. "Fear of what?"

He took a deep, settling breath, his expression serene and...happy. "I was afraid that if I let myself love again, I might lose you one day and it would hurt too much. And then I realized I was losing you anyway. I could let you go and avoid the pain, but I also would never know the exquisite joy of loving you. And I couldn't live without that."

"Oh, Jakob. Please don't say such things." She shook her head, her eyes filling with tears.

"It's true, Abby. I really mean it. Love comes with risks. But then I remembered my faith. *Gott* knows we won't grow without opposition in our lives. He wants us to live by faith. And how can I do that if I never need Him?"

"But what about Susan? You still love her."

"*Ach*, I do. And I think you wouldn't want me if I didn't. But I remember overhearing you speaking to Reuben the day you found your notes in his drawer. You told him that love can grow inside of you without reaching capacity. That love is eternal. It has no end. It just goes on and on. And right now, it has encompassed my heart. I love you, *liebchen*. Please, say you'll be mine forever. Because I can't go home without you."

"*Ahem!* Excuse me, miss, but the bus is boarding now. If you're going to Ohio, you better come now." The conductor stood in the doorway, waving at Abby.

A look of pure panic filled Jakob's eyes and the color drained from his face. He glanced between the conductor and Abby, as though his whole world were caving in on him.

"Please, Abby. Don't go." His voice sounded hoarse with emotion as he took her hand in his, looking deep into her eyes. "I understand now why my *vadder* wrote to you. He knew I needed you to heal my shattered heart. The bus must have broken down for a reason…to keep you here until I could arrive. *Gott's* hand is in this, I just know it. Stay and marry me. Please. Make me the happiest man in the world."

She hesitated, feeling torn. Wanting to believe him, but not quite daring to do so.

"If you go, I'll be forced to follow you to Ohio," he said.

She blinked in surprise. "You'd do that?"

He nodded. "I'll never give up until you accept my proposal. And believe me, you don't want me to meet up with Simon again. I believe in living a simple life without violence, but meeting with your *bruder* might push me to the breaking point. I won't allow him to hurt you again. And I mean it. I can't imagine living without you. I love you so much…"

"You'd really resort to violence if you saw Simon again?" She could hardly believe what he said. It was unthinkable, and yet the thought of Jakob defending her against her cruel brother touched her heart like nothing else could.

He looked down, his face flushed with shame. He nodded, staring at the floor. "*Ja*, I'm afraid so. *Gott* would be disappointed in me and I'd probably be shunned, but I'm afraid I might do Simon bodily harm if you go back to him. If my *familye* hadn't moved to Colorado when we were young, I would never have met Susan and would have married you years ago. I loved you even then, and I can't lose you again."

"Oh, Jakob!" Tears streamed from her eyes. She didn't even try to hold them back. "I... I love you, too. I have ever since I was a girl. That day you took the stick away from Simon and broke it over your knee, you were my knight in shining armor. I thought you were going to hit Simon, but you didn't. And in my eyes, you could do no wrong."

"Um, excuse me, but are you coming or not?" The conductor called to them again, sounding a bit irritated.

Jakob looked at her and waited, his face creased with hope and despair all at the same time. But she had to give him credit. He didn't answer for her. He waited, letting her decide for herself.

Abby shook her head, her heart near to bursting. "*Ne*, I'm not going. Would you be kind enough to reimburse my ticket instead?"

The conductor jerked his head toward the ticket office. "Sure. Just see Judith at the front counter and she'll help you with that."

Abby nodded and then she was in Jakob's arms. He held her close, gazing into her eyes with so much love and adoration that she wasn't sure she could contain it all. This was her dream come true. All she'd ever hoped for. To be wanted and needed.

To be loved.

"*Ach*, you've made me very happy. I love you so much," Jakob said.

"And I love you."

He kissed her and she was almost ashamed to admit that she didn't care who might see them. Almost. At this point in their relationship, she figured they'd both earned the right to a little show of romantic emotion.

When he released her, he smiled wide as he kept hold of her hand and picked up her suitcase and basket with his free hand. "Come on. Let's return your ticket, then stop off at Bishop Yoder's place on our way home. I want to receive his formal approval and let him know that we'll be holding a wedding at our place in the next couple of weeks."

"But that won't be enough time to invite Simon."

"*Gut*. I think it's best if he's not here. I don't want to give him the opportunity to interfere in any way."

Neither did she. "Do you think Bishop Yoder will agree to our marriage so soon?"

He nodded. "I do. He understands what is at stake. I believe he'll agree."

She smiled, unable to hide the exquisite joy radiating from her heart. "*Ach*, Naomi may not like it. We're not giving her much notice to plan the feast."

As they walked toward the ticket counter, he shrugged his unbelievably wide shoulders. "Don't you worry. She will be thrilled. And we'll help her."

"I doubt Simon will like it very much when the bishop writes to tell him that we have been married."

"I don't care what Simon doesn't like. He isn't a part of our lives anymore."

Yes, finally. Finally, she was well and truly free of her brother's abuse. Knowing Jakob was absolutely right, she didn't argue one bit. She waited patiently as he redeemed her ticket, then took her outside. He tied her suitcase and basket to the back of the horse, then helped her climb up behind him on the saddle.

As they rode down Main Street and headed out of town, she wondered what Bishop Yoder would say when he saw them riding together like this.

Wrapping her arms around Jakob, she spoke against the back of his neck. "It's not very modest of me to ride astride behind a man who isn't my husband."

He patted her arms, which were crossed in front of him. "I'm your betrothed now, which is almost as *gut* as being your husband. Before anyone can chastise us, we will be married. And Bishop Yoder will be too delighted by the news of our wedding to question our method of travel today. Especially when I explain the urgent reason why it couldn't be helped. When I'm old and gray, I'll tell our *kinder* that you were my runaway bride."

She snorted. "You make it sound so dramatic."

"It was, until I found you at the train station. I almost lost you. And now, I'll never let you go."

Accepting his word on the topic, Abby laid her cheek against his back and squeezed him tighter. It would do no good to argue the point, especially when she knew he was right. She'd achieved her fondest dream. She had Jakob's love. At that moment, nothing else mattered in the world except the two of them. The good Lord had brought them through. He'd brought them together. And that was all they needed.

* * * * *

Dear Reader,

Have you ever been abused, either verbally or physically? I'm guessing the answer is yes. We each have experienced abuse to some degree. Likewise, I believe we each are guilty of abusing others, whether by a harsh word or unkind treatment. But in this story, Abby's situation is quite serious. As a child and then a young woman, she didn't just suffer hurt feelings, but rather, she experienced daily severe abuse that scarred her both mentally and physically.

When someone has been the victim of long-term abuse, it becomes difficult for them to trust others. It can break their heart and spirit and lead to low self-esteem. I hope if you or someone you know is in this predicament, you will reach out for help, both from the Lord and also someone in a position of authority who can assist you in changing the situation. And if you are an abuser, please recognize that you need help, too.

God wants us to be happy. He wants us to reach our full potential and serve others with works of goodness. We cannot serve Him if we are in an abusive situation. Remember that you are a child of God. He loves you and you are of infinite worth.

I hope you enjoyed reading this story, and I invite you to visit my website at *www.LeighBale.com* to learn more about my books.

May you find peace in the Lord's words!
Leigh Bale

Get 4 FREE REWARDS!

We'll send you 2 FREE Books plus 2 FREE Mystery Gifts.

Love Inspired® Suspense books feature Christian characters facing challenges to their faith... and lives.

FREE
Value Over
$20

Get 4 FREE REWARDS!

We'll send you 2 FREE Books
plus 2 FREE Mystery Gifts.

Harlequin® Heartwarming™ Larger-Print books feature traditional values of home, family, community and most of all—love.

FREE
Value Over
$20

HOME *on the* RANCH

YES! Please send me the **Home on the Ranch Collection** in Larger Print. This collection begins with 3 FREE books and 2 FREE gifts in the first shipment. Along with my 3 free books, I'll also get the next 4 books from the Home on the Ranch Collection, in LARGER PRINT, which I may either return and owe nothing, or keep for the low price of $5.24 U.S./ $5.89 CDN each plus $2.99 for shipping and handling per shipment*. If I decide to continue, about once a month for 8 months I will get 6 or 7 more books, but will only need to pay for 4. That means 2 or 3 books in every shipment will be FREE! If I decide to keep the entire collection, I'll have paid for only 32 books because 19 books are FREE! I understand that accepting the 3 free books and gifts places me under no obligation to buy anything. I can always return a shipment and cancel at any time. My free books and gifts are mine to keep no matter what I decide.

268 HCN 3760 468 HCN 3760

Name _____ (PLEASE PRINT) _____

Address _____ Apt. # _____

City _____ State/Prov. _____ Zip/Postal Code _____

Signature (if under 18, a parent or guardian must sign) _____

Mail to the **Reader Service**:

IN U.S.A.: P.O. Box 1341, Buffalo, New York 14240-8531
IN CANADA: P.O. Box 603, Fort Erie, Ontario L2A 5X3

READERSERVICE.COM

Manage your account online!

- Review your order history
- Manage your payments
- Update your address

*We've designed the
Reader Service website
just for you.*

Enjoy all the features!

- Discover new series available to you, and read excerpts from any series.
- Respond to mailings and special monthly offers.
- Browse the Bonus Bucks catalog and online-only exculsives.
- Share your feedback.

Visit us at:
ReaderService.com